The Sad Eye

The Sad Eye

Bradd Burningham

GOOSE LANE

© Bradd Burningham, 1991

All rights reserved. No part of this work may be reproduced or used in any form or by any means, electronic or mechanical, including photocopying, recording, or any information storage and retrieval system, without the prior written permission of the publisher. Requests for photocopying of any part of this book should be directed in writing to the Canadian Reprography Collective, 379 Adelaide Street West, Suite M1, Toronto, Ontario, Canada M5V 1S5.

Published with the assistance of the Canada Council and the New Brunswick Department of Tourism, Recreation & Heritage, 1991.

The author wishes to acknowledge the support of the Banff School of Fine Arts.

Some of these stories have been previously published in the following magazines and anthologies: "The Girl with the Baby Arms" in *Saskatchewan Gold* (Moose Jaw: Coteau Books, 1982). "Four Poster" in *University of Windsor Review*, Vol. 22, No. 2, 1989. "Other Women" in *Generation* (University of Windsor), 1980 and in *More Saskatchewan Gold* (Moose Jaw: Coteau Books, 1984). "The Catch" in *Generation* (University of Windsor), 1979.

Cover painting: "Les dieux obscurs," by Max Ernst, 1957, oil on canvas, 89 cm x 116 cm, courtesy Museum Folkwang, Essen, Germany.
Back cover photo by Trudie Horodezky.
Book design by Julie Scriver.
Printed in Canada by Ronalds Printing.

Canadian Cataloguing in Publication Data

Burningham, Bradd, 1955-
  The sad eye

ISBN 0-86492-093-8

I.Title.

PS8553.U76S32 1991   C813'.54   C91-097556-6
PR9199.3.B87S32 1991

Goose Lane Editions
248 Brunswick Street
Fredericton, New Brunswick
Canada E3B 1G9

*To my parents and P.R., who believed.
And to J.B.*

the thing I came for:
the wreck and not the story of the wreck
the thing itself and not the myth
the drowned face always staring
toward the sun

> — Adrienne Rich,
> from "Diving into the Wreck"

Contents

9 The Girl with the Baby Arms

36 Realemon

46 Stag

63 Landlock

85 Four-Poster

93 Among Children

113 Stoneware

123 Other Women

139 The Sad Eye

166 The Catch

180 Something Is Coming

The Girl with the Baby Arms

It's fascinating, Henry. She draws them to her, to this place, a whole procession of virginal pilgrims. She and her arms — what there are of them.

They come from all over, these girls, though mostly from the grey, relentless business cities of northern Europe — Dusseldorf, Rotterdam, Birmingham. (I could show you, you know, on the globe; I'd spin it; you'd laugh, you silly bugger.)

They come, lured at first by the too-blue landscape of travel folders, enticed by inky-fingered, hoarse-voiced travel agents (I could do one for you; like Scrooge he'd be, remember?). They come looking for their simple Prince (Prince Valiant-like); or, the vaguer ones, for some tidy two-week packaged mystery.

And they find, at first, that the brochures haven't lied: that the sea and sky really are this colour; that the dull red of roof tiles and green of what trees there are, the brilliant white of sand beaches and white-washed cement buildings, come out of these gem-hard blues, are of them in the way that orange is of red and yellow; that this island does in fact have a chromatic logic of its own. (Look at the postcards I'm sending, Henry.)

Yes, this is what sets them up, this mere and not even intentional integrity of landscape. They differ from the ordinary run of tourists only in the degree of their hunger for it, something like it. And all are such innocents, really, greedy for . . . for what I don't know. Certainly not just for fun. For virtue, perhaps? Yes, maybe that. And their cities have made them all so damn literal-minded that they could well locate this vague longing in something as tangible as stones, a few trees. In their own maidenheads, for that matter. Not that I mean that last literally, of course. Quite the opposite, for the thing they make of this girl — Gothic heroine of the vestigial arms — is replete with a powerful, even overpowering sexuality. One of them even confessed to fantasies of caressing her arms, preferably while she slept. Is that sex? Maybe not, but all those I know of — practical girls these, "nice," and really virgins, more or less — have come prepared for it, with a variety of contraceptives (of the four I know of, three were on the pill; the fourth carried everywhere a box of three condoms). No, it's hardly chastity they want: the end of that is part of the reward. But something like it, as clean and simple an idea. Yes, virtue for sure, these modern day Pamelas, there's no other word, and in the form of something just as physical, just as true-blue as the scenes in the travel folders they always believed in, always set their fantasies in. That's what they're after, that's what they see in this girl. What sets them up for her. For me too, I guess, your lecherous younger brother. Let me describe her for you, Henry, and maybe you'll see what I mean.

No, let me go. *¡Déjeme en paz!*

I hear Wendy, you see (more of her later), rousing herself inside the flat, and I really should go down into town to market before she's up. She can probably use breakfast, poor girl.

But let me leave you in a place, rather than air. (Perhaps one of the Nursing Sisters could read this part to you, while you look at the cards? It will be my words at least, my rhythm. Maybe even the tone . . . Ah, Henry, it's so hard. Maybe I could finagle a camera from somebody.)

The Girl with the Baby Arms

Anyway, the flat itself is one of four set into a hill, tier-like, one atop the other. I am in the smallest and uppermost, and although the interior is a little claustrophobic — especially at the moment with an extra body about — my verandah is the whole roof of the flat below me. That's where I am now, and god, it's a good day, Henry. The white-washed stucco and cement brilliant like arc lamps almost, you can hardly look directly at them. The sky is cloudless; and yet it's cool up here on the hill, the bamboo mats spread and shading overhead. I can see a woman sunbathing topless on the roof of an apartment building down in the valley, must be a mile away, offering her breasts up to Sol. Between the two hotels on my side of the lagoon below (never could you call it a bay in this place) the water is so blue, it really is beyond believing: closing my eyes, it's almost as though the blue were burned onto the retina — abstracted blue it is, the feeling of blue. Yes, exactly like the travel folders.

And then, of course, across the lagoon is the facing range of hills, higher than mine, blunter and bleaker where they follow the bay around to the open sea. There is the richer side, with lower-lying three or four unit apartment buildings and some private summer houses interspersed.

Oh, and while I think of it, thanks for the card, Henry. Good to hear, especially after the long silence of... what is it? Three months? Did the Nursing Sisters help you buy it? I know you must be behind it though, somehow. Who else would have sent a postcard from that dreary industrial place, our town? Who would even have thought such things existed? And to send it here of all places, to this most exotic of Mediterranean vacation spots. I was glad anyway, Henry. Your writing is improving. You're being good, I know. Aunt Dorothy writes that they might start you learning a job at a workshop in the fall. Good. Just remember: IQ is a stupid myth, a bunch of blind numbers created by people like me to fill the empty spaces. You're Mensa where it counts, kiddo.

Are there any other cards besides the picture of the bridge over our brown river?

I'm back, Henry. Fresh bread, eggs and milk, my stomach warm from morning brandy with Rodriguez, the waiter in the café where I spend much of my time. It's a daily ritual (always excluding Sundays), my morning coffee and brandy with Rodriguez. *¡Dios mio!* he'll always say at some point during our conversation. He speaks passable English but somehow feels the exclamation doesn't translate well. *¡Diablos mio!* I'll get in some time after, titting for his tat. A good Catholic, Rodriguez — invariably the slightest look of disapproval will break through his impassive waiter's face, before we continue.

By this time I will have my brandy and coffee before me. Rodriguez's well-muscled haunches will be rested against the back of a chair at the next table. It will be too early for any of the hotel patrons or the summer apartment dwellers to be in the bar and too late for the few Spanish — mostly Rodriguez's relatives — who come for coffee just after he opens. It will be about nine-thirty. Rodriguez will have time for a regular of going on four months.

Somehow much of our conversation seems to consist of Rodriguez's sexual evaluations of the various *turistas* he meets at the cafe. Occasionally I contribute, if I happen to know the subject in question or if one fortuitously passes by. But primarily the discussions are lopsided, and usually soon turn to what Rodriguez chooses to reveal of his previous night's sexual exploits. The gallant waiter scrupulously avoids mention of any current names, for the good reason that most of his affairs, I am sure, are imaginary — although taken separately they are doggedly lacking in imagination, all are so similar. The women visitors to the island, mostly northern Europeans, don't go for the swarthy, short, heavily accented Rodriguez. His overtures, like those of other Spanish men I've seen, are too overt, his need too transparently

The Girl with the Baby Arms

great, in this country that only recently legalized even the softest porn.

So sometimes the conversation does become a little tiresome. But I don't really mind. Under pretence of swapping tales, I manage to get in the quota of chatter necessary to my own health, usually talking, provided I can think up enough sexual detail to justify it, about Brigitta and Johanna, two of the pilgrims I mentioned before, the first German, the second Dutch. Rodriguez even inadvertently supplied the name of another of their kind — this one before my time, her reputation therefore safe — Jennifer. She was the one with the mini-box of condoms (Rodriguez could never have invented a detail like that). Also, through careful attention, I sometimes find out a snippet or two of information about the people who interest me here, again inadvertently, for Rodriguez almost superstitiously avoids any talk of *her* (funny, almost nobody ever uses her name). As kind of a bonus for this general attentiveness I'm pretty sure I've discovered the dream beneath Rodriguez's almost professional *machismo:* to build a house on the property he already owns, marry the chaste señorita her parents have hidden away for him, and speak perfect English to his uncomprehending bride happily ever after. It doesn't have to make sense and I sympathize with him. I also make subtle use of this information as a lever whenever I feel the need to verbally reaffirm my own long-range plans. Periodically, say once a week, while Rodriguez salts away my money and forces his tongue around my non-British pronunciation, I will mention how very soon it is that I will be off to France to begin my intended year of language study, before returning home for good. Once again I will predict the ease with which I will be able to turn my thesis on Hemingway and Fitzgerald into a book; how it will almost certainly net me a good teaching job. As always, Rodriguez will indicate in a few words his own deep familiarity with Hemingway (no mention of old

Fitz), and with the conversation shifted back to him he will slyly guide it on to more usual topics. As for me, this is plenty — I'd rather not dwell on what for the moment isn't alive. (I really do need you, Henry, for the work to progress, it seems. It used to keep me honest, reading chapters of my thesis to you. No one could detect a bluff so surely as you, complain so uncompromisingly when I'd lose the rhythm, get tangled in my own words. You're a better scholar than others with treble the functioning grey cells, and much else besides.)

So this is how I start my mornings. Sometimes Rodriguez will join me in a brandy, on me of course (our poor parents' legacy dwindles, Henry, alas), and a first brandy and coffee will give way to a second and third, until the coffee is dispensed with altogether and the morning too. It's on such days (and I must confess this is one of them: it's nearly noon now) that I feel like a character from Conrad or Graham Greene, you know the sort — malingering, self-destructing on bad whisky in the shadows of decrepit open air bars, big slowly revolving ceiling fans barely disturbing the steamy air overhead. Punishing himself for some great guilt he must carry. It's a fun part to play, usually.

So, anyway, that's what I'm fresh from — brandy and talk of sex, and now thoughts of fictional guilt. The only real guilt I have is from not keeping closer tabs on you. And I'm redressing that wrong now, right?

Okay, let me get my thoughts in order for a moment. I know this is all unorganized (you should see — hear — the notes for my book). I've lost the habit of committing thought to paper, and with it, it seems, the skill. Although sometimes — this is just between me and you, Henry — sometimes it does seem like it's more than that, that my mind has taken on the colour of its environment. And you should see this one: the big pot that came with the kitchenette half-filled with butts — a whole quart, or is it a litre? of them —

The Girl with the Baby Arms

crumpled clothes and towels, the sofa bed unmade as it has been for, Christ (or should I say, *¡Diablos mio!*); anyway, seems like months. Empty now, the bed; I suppose Wendy must have returned to her hotel room while I was gone. And that's another thing: these girls I was talking about seem to expect it of me, seem to require a little of the chaotic before they go home, after what they think they have lost, or will lose, in this girl, in this place. But I'm not really like this, as you know, Henry. It's an affectation, an actor's job, and this step out of character the vacationer's prerogative, right? I really do need you here to tell me when I'm bluffing. But that's *why* I'm here, isn't it?

Where was I when I left you, then? I was going to tell you about Wendy — and the others, her European counterparts. Well, forget about them, the others. Rodriguez is right: nobody leaves much behind in this place, not even a reputation to sully. Maybe that's why it remains so clean, pure — it's so non-absorbent. And besides, theirs — my blonde-haired pair, Brigitta and Johanna — theirs were imperfect cases, their interest in *la chica* hardly more than flirtation. Theirs a short trip, and I the tour bus they transferred to only near the end, after the first inconveniently broke down.

But Wendy, yes there are still shards of Wendy's dream around, insistent as the fragments of Carthaginian artifacts they continually turn up here. Even my bed, the most resilient of furniture, has not had time to recover yet. Another two days and she'll be gone — her seven days here complete. After that I'm swearing off — you can ask Rodriguez.

That's where I first met her, Wendy that is, at the café, downing Cuba Libres way faster than was wise. Though I admit the meeting wasn't entirely an accident. I'd seen her before at the hotel disco, watched her intent on Alicia (there, I've said her name — curious how nobody but her family seems to, as though to say it were to take it in vain; Baby Arms, that girl, *la chica con los brazos*, usually just *her*). I knew already she was an English speaker (I'd heard her order a drink) and for once I wanted to speak to one of the pilgrims whose first language was my own. It was good I happened along, she needed to talk. A few more drinks and she might have become one of Rodriguez's adventures (maybe they are real; maybe we have more in common than I think).

As I was saying, I'm through with all that now. I can get back to my education. But I've paid special attention to Wendy's story — I want to chronicle it. A Case History, sort of. Vacation snapshots, to be gone over afterwards. To be shown family, the only ones possibly interested. To be shown you, Henry, my only remaining family.

Or — was it The Girl With The Baby Arms (Wendy's name for Alicia) I was going to describe first? It doesn't matter, they're both connected. To tell of one is to tell of the other, if I'm the one doing the telling.

Let me start with background information then. She's an American, Wendy, first of all, from some town in Michigan (just on the other side of the bridge in your picture, you know?). She works in a milk store, she says (really a variety store, like Nellie Belle's in our old neighbourhood). She's a big girl, dark-haired, full-bodied, with an unremarkable face but for sensual lips that smile too much, too aimlessly, when she drinks too much. But she's young yet, just about twenty I would say (a real youngster to you, eh kid?).

It started more than two years ago. (Two years ago: I would have been still doing course work in grad school, you still in day school. I'd visit home holidays, some weekends, to see you. Read to you. Mom and Dad as happy as they'd ever been — Dad drawing deep airy puffs on his pipe after his day at the office, Mom silently bustling around the house as she'd bustled all day selling clothes at Nancy's Shoppe. I wonder what she'd have thought of Wendy and the rest? I

The Girl with the Baby Arms

wonder where she was at eighteen?) Two years ago, anyway, I guess is as good a place to start it starting as any. Wendy would just have been leaving high school. Would have been hired on at the milk store, possibly was already working there part-time. Naturally it would just be a temporary thing, she'd have had her plans. By then she'd already have been watching her girlfriends getting hitched and pregnant, possibly even divorced, the boys, a year or two older, alternately settling into jobs to support this circle and getting scared out of them — all the closest mirrors going through the motions, the emotions, of adulthood, in short. It would be fine for them, she'd think, it would even be tempting. But no, she'd have her plans.

Working in the little store, she must have seen a lot in a short time. Every day her friends would come in, slightly older versions of her friends, *definitely* older versions, so similar and close together that she wouldn't be able to miss the continuum before her — all regularly picking up their bread and milk, living their lives seemingly on such a bland diet. It would make her uneasy, she'd need some sort of buffer to throw up between them and her. Something daily, too. Something she could touch, almost, like a lucky piece or a rabbit's foot.

She was lucky. She found a girlfriend who felt the same way. It probably kept her from giving up altogether or else folding down into that hard little shell of self where the desperation grows. So much is luck — and un-luck — accident, it seems. Anyway, between them they found more courage than either would have had separately. They decided to take a trip together, somewhere far, somewhere (probably Wendy who pushed for this) where they speak a different language.

That's how it started. Two teenagers saving for a few weeks in the sun: so many dollars in the bank, so many days until *the* day. Bankbooks and calendars, true things, things you could tape up next to the cash register if you wanted, feel through the cloth of your shop smock. They drew up the rules between them and stuck to them religiously.

And they did come, two years and some days later, changing planes at Barcelona for the island. Let me sketch out their itinerary for you from what I know or can guess.

Day one: They arrive mid-afternoon at the island airport. They are tired, jet-lagging, but settling into the seats of the hotel bus, the last connection made, they begin to relax out of their tight travellers' circle of immediate concerns. This happens, perhaps, during the first rumbling mile out from the airport. Gradually, they begin to notice their surroundings; are impressed and soothed by the passing countryside. For a short while they silently itch to tell each other of it, but cannot find the words: cannot immediately see how it is any different from, say, Michigan farmland. And then, slowly, it comes, the southern European ruralness of it: the olive orchards, the doll-sized stone-walled fields, terraced on the hills. They point out to each other the inevitable ageless women in black, the grizzled sun-black farmers, their counterparts, in the fields; the small stone farmhouses. And aware, they find more worthy of awareness: the two or three different languages being spoken around them separate out, stop being simply clamour, part of the general clamour their voyage has been. Everything begins to seem clear, becomes just as exotic as they imagined — more than they could have imagined. Although behind all this, trailing along at about the same speed as the bus, might be just the slightest apprehension that it is all going to stop, perhaps when the bus does.

But it doesn't. They arrive at the beachside hotel, depart from the cool shadowiness of the bus — and I have already described this scene to you, Henry. They look down over the

The Girl with the Baby Arms

lagoon, the beach (the bus is always parked to afford the best possible view of these), and decide that despite tiredness, before even dinner, they have to go for a swim. And they do: ineffectually trying to hustle the bellboy up ahead of them to their room, pulling swimsuits from the bottom of suitcases, barely noticing their lodgings; hurrying down to mingle with the exotic near-naked bodies, the bright beach cots and umbrellas; watching with equal awe the rented sailboards slipping crosswind in front of the beach and the smooth dark waiters mixing drinks and building sandwiches in the slight shade of the snack huts.

After that, up again in their rooms, shaking sand from their swimsuits, giggling, each surreptitiously smoothing sea salt over tingling pale skin, they dress, and still not completely unpacked, descend again for dinner in the big hotel dining-room.

Daringly they choose from the two or three set menus, marvel over the seafood that neither would have been keen to eat only days ago; over the yellowish woody-tasting white wine so different from the whisky and Coca-Cola of their experience.

Up in their room again, now fully into their second winds, they change a third time, decide on a drink downstairs — oh, at least one — before bed.

Downstairs they see the action going on around them or at least feel the promise of it in the lobby air. Are reminded by signs or the desk clerk of the disco in the basement which starts at eight.

And so down they go, through the door to something from a televised dream it must seem, picking their way through the pulsing, darkened below-ground room, the main light coming from the glittering, faceted ball revolving over the dance floor, to find a seat.

It is here, during the next half hour or so, where Wendy's friend Mary Ellen meets her companion for the next six days.

She is lucky — he is just beginning his stay there too. He asks her to dance in his British boy's voice, and so it goes, the whole week-long romance — the maximum period — set to the tune of that single loud and endless song. *Their* song, they decide.

And Wendy, how is it for her that first night? Let me tell you, as near as I can construct it.

I can see her watching her friend up on the dance floor with her soon-to-be lover. She is, maybe, a little envious. But not much. They have been there so briefly that anything is still possible — another British boy, something even better. No hurry. She checks over her surroundings: dazzled by the sea, the foreign languages, the plane rides, the bare fact of the trip itself, she welcomes a chance to settle into a setting of her own — any setting. Lazily she lets herself be transfixed by the reflective sphere over the dance floor and the periodic strobe lights, freezing the dancers into series of snapshots. Enjoys the peace of the overloud disco music, so much like silence. It is the perfect time for her: a prolonged single moment, ending with her looking out over the groups of other patrons — handsome, tanned people from a fairyworld of other nations, athletically straining their mouths to talk over the music, or contentedly laid-back, sipping drinks — looking out over these and knowing them to be her own people, whenever, at her leisure, she chooses it to happen; knowing too that it doesn't have to happen yet. Finally, though, it is another choice she makes: her eyes stop at one particular table of people, focus on the one person who clearly is the focus of the rest of the table — and there they stay for the rest of the week, for the rest of her life, up until now.

It is hard for me to describe what Wendy's first impression must have been like for her, Henry. When I first met Alicia, I thought her scatter-brained, dynamic perhaps, and possibly a little charismatic, if that word can be applied to a woman. But I didn't detect anything overwhelmingly remarkable in that dark-eyed, tightly packaged body. Even her arms — they do look like baby arms, not deformed, just undeveloped; usually hanging by her sides to about breast level — even these seemed nothing special, I guess since thanks to you I am used to those not quite of the standard model. It's important to see it through Wendy's eyes, though. Maybe you can see it better that way than I?

So, back to the disco. Wendy's first sight of Alicia a series of snapshots — the strobe light starting up just as she catches sight of her. Alicia's hair a cascade of black water frozen in mid-air as she flips it from side to side (she does it purposely, in imitation of American fashion models), her white cottony dress brilliant in the arc-white light, subduing the frozen-as-they-mill other whites around her; a cigarette enormous between her tiny fingers, the arm fully extended as she brings it to her mouth; and finally the whole-heartedness of that wholly open mouth (the only thing I have known her to give away and her best quality) in its soundless — to Wendy — laugh. And around her her entourage, intent on her, focused on her as I have already said: her brother, his German girlfriend, a couple of others from the apartment buildings on the opposite side of the lagoon, her paid companion Julie from Perth, a shy Australian girl — Alicia the centre of their attention, animatedly orchestrating the dancing room around her, yet so above it all. A single, sinewy muscle, effortlessly and constantly flexing. Dependent on these, it must be obvious (how much so Wendy wouldn't guess; I would have); yet who would dare to brush the hair from this girl's eyes when it becomes hung up on a brow, or offer to raise the glass she struggles two-handed to her mouth? Who would risk a sting from that arm occasionally flicking like a snake's tongue to dislodge ashes from her cigarette? Yes, a strong-willed beauty who has every excuse not to be — anything. Who could be nothing. And who could blame her?

So Wendy spends the rest of the night at the disco, watching The Girl With The Baby Arms. Just watching. Mary Ellen and her new friend come back to the table between dances, are solicitous; but they have seen Wendy turn down offers to dance and she hasn't suggested to Mary Ellen they return to the room — and besides, Mary Ellen must decide, it's her vacation too — so they let her be.

Meanwhile, at several points, Wendy must discover she has finished her drink, and so goes to the bar, reserving her seat with her handbag, for another of the hotel's tired Cuba Libres.

And it is at this point, or one of them — one of the later ones judging by Wendy's uncertain gait — where I come in. I am at the bar drinking lemonade — the liquor at the hotel is way overpriced — surveying the latest batch of Packaged. (I have come down from Rodriguez's to give my feet something to do. I have come down to think the same tired thoughts: that I am long overdue in France. That I have spent much longer than I ought to have in this tourist trap of a place. I am thinking of you, Henry, about the ten thousand dollars I have left in the bank at home and how it might best be spent. I am thinking about the two girls I stumbled upon by accident, Johanna and Brigitta, who spent hours telling me in broken English of their dreams, of the loveliness of this place, and of the most amazing girl they'd seen — did I really know her? I am watching Alicia flirting with the overweight Belgian at the table next to her who claims to be writing a history of the island.) I see Wendy, anyway, come to the bar, order another drink and return none too steadily to her table to continue mooning at Alicia. She eventually has two more drinks, I two more lemonades. By then she is cozily drunk and has solidly formed in her mind whatever impression it is that will take the rest of the week and me and an unfortunate lapse on the part of Alicia to demolish.

It is almost midnight on Monday.

That night in bed Mary Ellen talks forever about (what

else could he be called?) Arthur. Then she goes to sleep, leaving Wendy to stay awake all night listening to the sea. (In reality, Wendy herself falls asleep and dreams she hears the sea, if that, for the lagoon is a still place, except during storms, insofar as I know it and I know it pretty well. In fact, I think I was actually at the beach that night, after Rodriguez's place closed down — around four, I think, after the disco too had closed and Alicia and company had left for the night. No sea sounds.)

Day two: Mary Ellen runs into Arthur in the dining-room at breakfast. They re-establish connection and decide to go down to the beach together, leaving Wendy behind with a second cup of coffee to follow along later.

Wendy decides to walk up the hill to town to look through the shops. This does not take long, for there are surprisingly few shops designed to appeal to tourists, these mostly run by the summer residents. She takes a fast look at pottery, some leather goods, rattan bags and so on and soon lands at Rodriguez's with another coffee before her. She does not feel like the beach quite yet. She does not remember Rodriguez especially, which I suppose is a mark of his professionalism.

Wendy, perhaps unwittingly, has chosen one of the two or three best tables at the café, in the open air part near the street. Prime observation spots, they front the main bus stop in town — at times, *become* the main bus stop. Rodriguez picks up a lot of business this way, from people waiting or watching. Wendy doesn't get a chance to observe very long, however, for this is a day Alicia has chosen to rise early and go into La Ciudad to meet a boyfriend. She approaches the café at the latest possible moment, with Julie and to the confusion of Wendy, who spills the expresso she isn't liking very much anyway. Unlike Mary Ellen with Arthur, Wendy has no connection to re-establish with Alicia. The best she can think to do is board the bus with the others when it arrives, dumping all her coins into the smiling bus driver's hands.

On the bus she takes a seat near the rear, behind the two girls she has followed, without the vaguest idea where she is going. For twenty or so kilometres, she still has no idea where she is going, despite the fact that the identical terrain of the day before — the essence of all she dreamed possible then — is passing by. But it *is* the same route: she marvels now as she did then. Marvelous, to be able to watch for all those kilometres: Alicia's posture almost regal when she is silent and motionless, her hair so airily light in the breeze from the open windows; her neck, the long cool dryness of it, the taut smooth cords when she bends to say something to her companion — such a superb neck, compared to the smudged and pudgy damp ones of her neighbours. Marvelous too, the gauzy cotton of her dress's shoulder straps, the slope of her narrow shoulders so tantalizing above the shielding back of the bus seat. And finally, the most marvelous thing of all: the simple fact that Wendy has not dreamed her into existence in the first place (unspoken here: that she is not simply a freak outside the circus disco world). For twenty kilometres or so Wendy is content with this, although at the same time is looking ahead, yearning to touch her: inventing scenarios in which she will brush against her when exiting the bus, or no, will save her from tripping as they descend the stairs to wherever they are going, wherever Alicia is taking her.

But then the trip is almost over, Wendy begins to recognize the highway past the airport, and the — the crest? — of the event has been reached. It is not that anything disastrous happens yet: Wendy's vision, version, fictionalization, call it what you want, of The Girl With The Baby Arms grows, is reinforced, even as it is under assault, even as the final demolition occurs. It is only the ease of belief that ebbs and flows and is at this point, Henry — to continue with the wishy-

The Girl with the Baby Arms

washy metaphor — about as high up on the one shore as it is possible to be.

And so, at one point, responding to something that Julie says, Alicia laughs her glorious laugh — which carries easily to the back of the bus and thrills Wendy more than can any of the passing scenery. But she *says* something, in a corresponding volume; and in a language that is unmistakably English. And for some reason, up until now, Wendy has never considered her as someone who communicates through normal speech. (Of course she never forms this precise thought, just as she never described Alicia in quite the words I use here. But she has endowed her with a suitably vague nationality — Swiss or Austrian or Lithuanian . . . or something, anything: generously let her be a citizen of any country far enough away and with a language of which she knows not a word. And this amounts to the same thing.) So when the girl turns and does say something to her companion in clear English, Wendy is surprised, and, somehow, hurt. Also a little embarrassed, for at the same moment Alicia is being transformed into something very normal (in other words, someone altogether too much like Wendy herself), she turns even further in her seat and Wendy is never quite sure whether Alicia has caught her staring eye or not. She shifts it to the passing roadside after that.

Wendy can never remember what it is Alicia has said, although she definitely has heard; she tries to recall then and afterwards and even suggests possibilities to herself. But the words are lost, swept out the open window into the dirty outskirts of La Ciudad just as they enter them.

(Last night she claimed to have heard them in her sleep, but true to form, I think she was confusing her dreams with reality. It stormed last night: I think she heard the sea.)

Wendy never intentionally gets so close again.

When they get to town, Alicia is met by one of her boyfriends on a motor scooter. Wrapping her infant arms around his shoulders, the two of them buzz off, leaving Julie to whatever errands, real or diversionary, and Wendy to kill time until the next bus.

Day three: Wendy goes to Rodriguez's café immediately after breakfast at the hotel. She has two cups of coffee (*café con leche*, this time). She sees me sitting at my usual place, waiting for Rodriguez to finish serving her. She heads back towards the hotel, perhaps goes down to the beach. An hour later she is back. Then gone again to I don't know where.

It is not until later that evening that she sees Alicia. Before that she is restless as during the day: between eight and ten she is up and down between the disco and her room at least three times. At ten she descends again to the basement level, but before entering the disco proper stops at the washroom in the corridor. Combs her hair. Within the stall next to the mirror she hears the murmur of voices, sees two pairs of feet beneath the edge of the door, at least one pair of which she recognizes; through the crack, a flash of white cottony material.

She goes up to her room again. Lays down without turning on the light. Much later, Mary Ellen comes in with Arthur, and they lay together on Mary Ellen's bed, occasionally giggling, possibly fully-clothed. Wendy pretends to be asleep. In the dark she fantasizes usurping Julie's place as Alicia's companion. She imagines helping her dress for bed at night; caressing her hair after she falls asleep. Imagines protecting her from people like herself, rude intruding people who are disconcerted by four legs in a toilet stall.

Day four: The vacation is wasting away. Wendy, a sensible girl, can see this. She knows it is fruitless to be following around an English girl who happens to have a pair of funny

The Girl with the Baby Arms

arms. She goes on a bus excursion with Mary Ellen and Arthur to another part of the island for shopping. She buys a leather change purse for her mother, a straw bag such as all the islanders carry for herself. After they return they go to the café in town, the three of them; it is considered a great find by the other two, who have spent their time exclusively at the beach, in the hotel, and in one another's arms. I see the three of them there, having drinks. After a time the other two go on ahead to the beach. I go over to Wendy's table and by way of introduction offer up my nationality; it is the first time we have actually met, though she remembers seeing me there before. After this we establish our names, and our occupations, more or less (I tell her I am a student on my way to France; which is true, though why it sounds like a gigolo's boastful lie I'd rather not think). And since I know the subject which would most interest her — and like everyone I want to be interesting, the highest virtue there is, I am coming to believe — I lead the conversation around to, first, some gossipy talk of the summer people of the island, and then, naturally, to Alicia.

I give her the answers to the few questions she can think to ask about Alicia's status on the island, her family and social set, where she lives in England. I help her frame her responses to my questions (I have after all had some experience myself as a listener) and gain much of the information I have just used to document her particular version of obsession with — The Girl With The Baby Arms. She uses this term haltingly, embarrassedly, the first time. But I encourage her, use it myself, and soon this is the name she uses for Alicia. It is the most original thing this girl says; and frankly, Henry, I am a little disappointed at this point by her. I expect more, I think, hearing the story from someone supposedly fluent in my own tongue. Nonetheless, it is the same story I have been interested in right along; and it is almost comforting, the familiarity of it.

Pointing out my little *casa* on the hill, I invite Wendy to come up to continue the discussion. But it is now that she must notice the bagginess of my knee-torn jeans, my shapeless Indian cotton shirt — none too clean — and the scruffiness of my ten-day-old beard (my full one having been cut off about that many days ago in yet another unacted-on decision that it was time to move on). Now that she must decide that I, although no shorter than she, am really very likely a not-very-cleverly-disguised troll, with who knows what intentions once I lure her up to my hillside lair. She turns down my offer of another Cuba Libre (I've already bought her three) and claims a prior commitment on the beach.

I'm afraid you'll have to hang on for a minute, Henry. I have to stop for a while — as I have been anyway all afternoon, for intermittent verandah pacing, drinks, and even once for a swim. But now at least I have a good reason. A messenger approacheth — Alicia's brother huffing up the endless steps of my hill (Northerners were never made for this climate, Henry). I'll be distracted for a while. We're almost at the end now, anyway.

It's night now, Henry. It's a bit chilly. A billion stars are out, a spectacle you only see — I've only seen at least — in unindustrialized areas near the sea. Though even where you are, you'd still see the brightest of them, I think. On a clear night would still find the same constellations. A billion hard, so hard, points of light, the model so poorly reproduced by the disco's shiny sphere. So many needles of light required to support this other, larger, more garishly painted globe. You'd see them I guess several hours before — or is it after me, I don't remember. And of course that's what separates us too, the slow revolving of the Earth.

Do you remember, Henry, when we were young, when I was in the Cub Scouts? I tried to show you the constellations — the big and little dippers, Cassiopeia, Orion, I don't remember what else, don't even remember where to look for all of these. I knew then though, and we both tried and tried, but you just couldn't fill in the lines between the dots in the sky, like those games that I loved and you could never do either. It didn't matter. I gave you a hug (no problems there, you were always a handsome boy, easy to love, my tall fair-haired older brother; between us we could have added up to something). Then we went inside, and that was the first time I read you a story, something Dad had always done before. I remember the story because it was one I'd never liked very much myself: *The Three Little Pigs*. Pigs were always so grey in the storybooks, and so dirty in real life — uninspiring animals — and we lived after all in a real brick house. Years before, before I counted myself too old for nursery stories, I went in for complicated tales of dragons and princesses. But this was your favourite.

That was our experience with stars, Henry. The other stars I remember were those in the sky the night Mom and Dad died. Years and hundreds of story-readings later. There weren't so many stars in the sky then as here now, but it was a crisp winter night, the temperature way below zero, and they were such clear pinpricks as I drove the two hundred miles home from school. It was such a perfect black and those stars seemed so far away. As I left the parking lot, after Aunt Dorothy phoned with the news, the snow was only an inch or so deep and it crunched like that foam taffy candy we used to get from Nellie Belle's. I remember thinking then, how could a car slide in such snow? It seemed so dry, a million miles away sparkling on the ground. How could Dad, such a careful helmsman, lose control of a car driving on such distant sandpaper? But of course it was warmer, the snow heavier, cloying, by the time I got home. Aunt Dorothy was up when I got there and you were in bed. Tearful and afraid, she hadn't told you. That was left for me. The cooling bodies down at the hospital, left for me. And all I could think was, how was I going to explain to you about snow?

Anyway, Henry, it's night, as I was saying. You're catching up to me, the Earth is revolving faster. Below us I can see a few windows lit haphazardly in the two hotels and in the apartment buildings across the lagoon. I was about to tell you about last night.

Last night I stayed in my flat. I had my big shutter doors closed to the night and the temptations of Rodriguez's. I was boning up on *le subjonctif.* I think it was quite late. I had slept in the afternoon, so I wasn't tired. I would say it must have been sometime past three when she, Wendy, came.

Apparently she had gotten too close again. Far too close this time. The vacation was finished, I could tell that. And the inevitable route followed by all the pilgrims — the one sometimes ending up on the stairs cut into my hill — well, her variation turned out to be the most dramatic of all.

I found out, over glasses of cheap purple wine, the only thing I had left to drink, that she had followed Alicia yet again to the disco. That more than this, she had grown bolder since I'd last seen her at the café and had decided to follow her home. She wanted to see where Alicia slept (where the baby slept, I wanted to say for her), as though this was going to resolve something.

So she followed Alicia from the disco — so preoccupied with her that she ignored the possible significance of her escort, neither paid companion nor brother. Followed, staying far back, always outside the outposts of light leading away from the hotel down to the lagoon beach. She already knew the general direction they would have to go, around the lagoon to the other shore — I had told her. And she wanted to leave them, or at least *her*, their isolation, while sharing in it at the same time — don't ask me the logic of it, I'm only a reporter. So she observed, watched their inevitable veer down to the edge of the water, his arm around her waist, hers fully extended along his nearest shoulder. Nearly motionless, she watched until she lost them in the shadows of the small stand of pines at the far end of the beach. And then, afraid she might lose them altogether, she began running, high up on the beach to avoid the reflected light of the water, losing a sandal along the way. Probably it is fortunate that what happened did before she reached them — she thought they had continued walking — or else she might literally have stumbled upon them grittily contorting, at who knows what consequences considering her high-strung state. Although it might have been better for Alicia if she had; she has a good sense of humour. It might even have been better for me.

But it didn't work out that way. Running through the sand, about half-way around the lagoon, the scene jolting as though seen from inside a movie camera, Wendy saw a white figure rise from the ground at the foot of the pines, heard either herself or it sighing with the effort. Then it was off, running across her field of vision towards the water, breaking out of the shadows into the moonlight. It was only then, stopped herself, that Wendy made any sense of what was going on, the naked blurred body skimming along the line of surf like one of the rented sailboards, dark hair flying, abbreviated wings waving in the air, clipped wings, like those of some ground bird building for a flight remembered only in its genes. She ran like that for a few minutes, up and down the surf — Wendy said it was awful, the way she staggered, unbalanced, powerless to cover herself, but I suspect she decided that only afterwards. She couldn't have known then a different version of Alicia was about to predominate. At the time it must have been beautiful, Wendy ready to soar with her, even at the very moment — her practical self-protectiveness coming into force — she was wondering if the girl needed help, if her friend perhaps shouldn't be helping her off that winter-like stage of moonlight on a sand-snow field.

It did end in awfulness, for everyone, so perhaps Wendy did sense what was about to happen. Moving deeper and deeper into the dark silver-tinted water, the runway shortening, Alicia slowing with each pass, she finally bogged; dropped splashing to her knees; her arms scuttling the air like seashells' pedicles. Then fell face forward, gulping sea. It took a moment, but the soft uneven crying noises finally rose from her compact belly, came messily sobbing out on a small stream of saltwater. Reached Wendy on shore. Who knows what the immediate reason? Maybe because she was no more able to swim than fly. Who could blame her?

So that was it, Henry, another one down. I think I'm talking about Wendy.

I can't really say how they find their way here, but somehow they seem to, the victims. They think I'm sympathetic or something — though hardly *simpático*, that's not it. They see my life with you written all over me, I think. See themselves, too, of course. Waking from the ruins of their dreams see not a gem perhaps, but a rough-edged fragment of mirror among the breakage — something, anyway, to reach for.

So, another one. Another night in my unweeded bed. My last, I think, or nearly. Time for France and some clean, cold rote-work, studying the language I've set myself to understand and to speak. I know you think I could stand some brushing up on my first one, some of that Three-Pigs clarity applied, but that's the way it goes. There's never going to be such perfect order in my life or my words, you'll have to get used to it. Oh don't worry, your clever brother who you always trusted to know the end of stories will be home again, just as per plan. I wouldn't leave you locked up forever in the Evil Tower, a prey to the sympathies of Aunt Dorothy and your black and white sitters, the rigorous Sisters. I'm no fool, I know my original stars, though fewer and dimmer at home than those that seem to be here, are the only ones I truly get to work with. I know this time in the sun, the lovely mess of it all, is just a vacation, all this just the vacationer's prerogative. I don't forget the night, your strong arms around me and my head on your chest, as we blubbered together about snow.

And yet there is still the note, delivered by Alicia's brother, to contend with. Alicia, it seems, has arranged that I can come stay with her and her family for as long as I wish in England. She is a spoiled daughter, and her father, well, rich. He thinks I am good for her, whether my intentions be completely honourable or not. He has connections and there are strong suggestions of a decent teaching job if I decide to come.

Let me describe one final scene for you.

Atop the cool damp sheets of my mangled bed:

Two fetal hands, perfect in themselves, resting level with breasts slightly flattened and small, though almost mothergodly in comparison to the hands. The breasts, however, are slung low on the hard cage of ribs, and the hands cannot quite reach them. It is now, during this scene more than any other time, that I can see what the others saw — her infantile hands kneading, caressing her own woman's breasts, she a parent to her own childish, onanistic self-infatuation, a child to the mother. Subject and object. Such a perfect image of self-containment. Yes, for the first time I almost saw what they saw in her and what she in a way needed to see too. Those moments, I can almost guarantee it, marked one of the few times in her short sensualist's life when she ever completed something significant totally unassisted. Or so, somehow, I allowed it to seem. Yet, she had needed me, if only as midwife, possibly as witness. It was such a small service to perform, raising those breasts to her hands.

But it was a vital one, both she knew and I, proof that it was all a performance. And of course the rest of our time together was never like that, except in that it too was a performance, although of another kind. By then I had already spent much of my summer with her, either here at night or with her whole family around their superfluous apartment pool during the afternoons; was already providing far greater services than the one I mentioned, a few of them non-sexual, those she didn't gladly suffer from even her family or Julie. It had been months then since I'd first met her at a party on her side of the lagoon and she'd followed me back here. I was tired and more than a little drunk, I remember the night: a friend dropping her off his buzzing, bulbous-bodied motor scooter like a white larva at the foot of my hill, me watching her from a chair on the dark verandah, growing a notch more weary with each step she took. All I wanted to do then was go to bed, which is of course what she had in mind too. And that night she surprised me, bucked me for all she was worth, and with the floor drunkenly heaving, a spectrum of colours unattached and swirling around us, we were satyr and virgin, I the parasitic eel to be shook from between her legs. Then we switched roles and god, that willful mouth, so hard and skilled, then that feral laugh. The services I performed then and after were hardly small, but then again neither were hers for me: we turned that fetid goat's den upside down, sweated, rutted, drooled, shat on the walls, cast anything like dignity aside, and for a good long season pretended there was neither head nor foot to my tired daybed. It was just what I needed.

Yes, for a while we played at being what we needed to be, played at seeing or not seeing what the other needed us to see or not see. Played so well we forgot who was whom, forgot we were playing, simply forgot.

I told her once that, maybe, someday, I'd come to London to visit the Queen.

And now, mired by something in the night sea water, she really wants me to.

Aunt Dorothy says our rooms are clean and waiting whenever we want them, Henry.

And yes, I will be coming home, soon.

R<u>ealemon</u>

Feb. 7

"Women In Chains." We're in Arsenault's Video and there's all these tapes with Party and Night and Heat in the title. Adult section, top shelf near the back, I thought it was new but Wilf says it was always there. Where good people don't notice and kids can't reach. So who rents them I'd like to know. Small town like this you can guess who'd like to but you'd think they'd be too embarrassed walking up to Donna Filmore's daughter or even old Arsenault himself with one of those in their hand. Only ones I can think wouldn't care are Dormers. Men in chains would love to watch women in chains, even the queers, and they wouldn't give a damn who knew.

Wilf says they're mainly for stags.

Ended up with "Aliens" cause Wilf and Jamie wanted it. Blood and guts all over. Little reptile monsters bursting out of people's chests. Almost made Wilf turn it off except Jamie wasn't scared at all. Spent a lot of time in the kitchen making popcorn and Jamie and Wilf never had such good waitress service for pop and beer. Didn't have any butter on mine.

Realemon

Sunday, 8th

Bad dreams last night from that movie. Then woke up with that stupid song running in my head. Are you sleeping? Are you sleeping? Singing the words round my toothbrush and even when I stopped the tune stayed.

Dormez-vous? Dormez-vous?
Sonnez les matin-a
Sonnez les matin-a
Ding dong ding

Two years now working at that place and trying to wean myself off that song for a year and a half most of. Kind of thing sticks in your head then just won't go. Why'd they have to call it Dormier? Just because the town's Dormier didn't mean they had to call the Pen that too.

The Big House
The Joint
The Big Sleep
Le Grand Dorm-something

Sounds like a 1940s movie. Bette Davis starring.

Dormier, dormant, doors
Sleepers

Shivered when I wrote that just now, Sleepers. Makes it worse somehow thinking of the inmates like that, an innocent word like the song, hiding so much evil. Like one of those alien things burrowing around inside something sweet and innocent, a little kid or

Ooh. Triple shiver, creepy skin. Bad luck to even write stuff like that about kids.

Feb. 12th

Had an awful day.

This morning at the gate Ven decides I'm due for a spot-check. Goes through my purse starting with my wallet the way they always do. Holds up a handful of bills. Doesn't say anything, just holds them up.

Tell him sorry, grocery day, which is the truth. You're not supposed to have more than twenty dollars on you inside.

Then he holds up my diet pills.

Guess I'll just take three I say, covering up since I don't need any, maybe one or two. You're not supposed to carry more than a day's dose of pills either, even 222s. Would have been embarrassed, diets are embarrassing, I don't know why, but I knew even worse was coming.

My B.C. pills. Pink plastic package with that fancy little cameo picture stamped on it. Looks like a make-up case from a toy purse and pills the size of saccharin tablets — keep me sweet which I definitely would not be if I got pregnant right now. Way he holds it you'd think he'd get pregnant himself just touching the case. Probably against his religion or something.

Was going to explain about going to the drugstore tonight after groceries. I needed the prescription label pasted on the package. But the way he held them — those shiny brown fingers of his pinching that little pink case — it made me mad. Like they were contraband he'd found in the toilet bowl. When it's *his* fingers always look like they've been dabbling in shit.

What's next? I tell him. You want I should drop my pants, touch my toes?

Didn't know an Indian guy could blush. This one sure

Realemon

did. Made a big production of *not* watching me when I put the money and stuff in my lockbox. Probably report me.
Day went downhill from there.

Mon. Feb. ?

Wilf says there's talk of layoffs at the shop. Told him he'd just have to open up his own shop with the machines he's already got, start small, treat it like an ordinary job. Not like last time, up till 2 watching tv then sleep till noon. He's always wanted to. Course he'd get the U.I. for a year.

Jamie told us about this littler kid at school who's been trying to pick a fight with him. Wilf said just boot him in the ass, tell him come back when he grows up. But the kid's not *that* much smaller, I know him so does Wilf. Wilf has a hard time shrinking down to Jamie's size sometimes, understanding how his mind works. Situation like this Jamie's going to lose whether he wins loses or walks. Tell him walking's smartest, the way a mother should, but think in my heart it might be better if he fought.

Feb. 20

They're trying the Realemon again which scares the hell out of me. Must've been a movie or tv show on lately with it.

Last time it happened, year and a half ago, got so bad I knew the contraband reports were in before I even sat down. Smell of lemon pie coming off the reports with the clipped on confiscated/found papers. That was just after my probationary period ended and I never thought anything of it, thought someone must have been keeping the reports with their lunch. Weeks before I mentioned it to anyone and then we all got hell. Turned out the same thing was happening with outgoing mail except Kroger smokes too much, he'd never notice. Had to go back through every c/f doc in the file, by then you couldn't tell by sniffing. Our thumbs all burned from holding Bic lighters and finally they brought in the portable oven. Then the Realemon raids, they confiscated two bottles, half a dozen plastic lemons, took the fruit juice out of the Canteen and for two months wouldn't allow any citrus fruit in the kitchen.

It's funny. Ordinarily that's the part of the work I like, it's even fun, checking the c/f docs for hidden meanings and not so hidden. Straining your eyes over little slivers of paper that turn up in library books, ironing out crumpled cigarette packages and candy wrappers inmates have got caught passing to each other, or just deciphering notes the guards find in cells or on the floor. Once the librarian even sent the book along too because the note looked like a code. It's like a puzzle and you have to use your imagination. A Pen's an anthill, they've got just one mind between them, not smart but big, and you have to figure out what it's thinking one day to the next. That's what Kroger said my first day on the job and it's true kind of. It's just the invisible writing that bothers me and I could see my hand shaking today taking the papers out of the oven, waiting for the words that might be there. Heat cooks the lemon juice brown and there's something especially evil about brown writing.

Course even when you find stuff it's ordinarily just about drugs and different deals and gang business.

But that first time on one of the notes it was different.

Tro says do Cormier.

I remember each word and the handwriting too. Remember it so clear I could write that handwriting if I had to, like drawing a picture. Remember it cause I knew Cormier, he used to sing to me when he swept our floor. *Tro says*

Course by the time the note got read Cormier was dead.

I've never written this before, feel so bad about it I only wanted to forget. Almost quit then except we needed the money. And when I first got the job Wilf said, Internal Intelligence, good place for you cause you're so smart. And he meant it.

Is it any wonder I love that man?

26th

Been doing outgoing mail this week cause Kroger's sick. Checking the addressees are on the list and opening up most of the stuff from particular inmates. Mr. Boychuk said open the letters to lawyers too, be careful. We're not supposed to but lots of times they're just getting their lawyers to forward stuff. Got monthly reports to type too.

Mar. 4

They've been saying there's something in the air this last week or so. A couple of the guards and the Clerk III Brenda. Didn't notice any tingling myself though till today.

In stories you read about people sensing danger in the air and the hair on the back of their neck pricking up. Always thought that was just made up till I came here.

Felt it today. Had to walk over to the Shops Office to check a report and as soon as I stepped in the yard I felt it. The hair on my neck and a burning feeling like I had to pee. A long walk through that yard, eyes going all the time. Checking for the scuffle that's really a diversion, the inmate veering towards you or away from you, the littlest move out of the ordinary. You can't see up into the towers but I could feel the guys up there watching every step.

Stayed at the Shops Office killing time watching the monitors for the different shops till a guard could escort me back. Got Walley. Nobody's sposed to know who they are, but Walley's a co-ordinator on IERT, the SWAT team. One of the few non-rotating members. He never said anything, but the way we walked we split up the territory, me checking the right him the left. Felt if I even blinked something bad might happen. I kept bumping into his shoulder.

I've probably broken a law by writing that down about IERT.

Anyway that's how I knew there was something in the air.

Jamie came home with a black eye. He didn't want to talk about it not even to Wilf.

Mar. 5

Phoned Mr. Teed at school today and he didn't know anything about a fight.

Went to watch Jamie play hockey after school with Wilf. He high-sticked a kid when the ref wasn't looking, no need for it, puck nowhere around. The kid went down and had to be helped off the ice. Some of the other parents booed. Wilf balled him out in the car, turned out the other kid didn't even *say* anything to him. Jamie just sat there saying yes, no, don't know and that made Wilf madder. Wanted Wilf to stop but he was probably right.

Mar. 7

Another movie tonight. Told them no more "Aliens" so we got a comedy. "Beverly Hills Cop" which I thought would be okay but it wasn't. Hero's this black guy who used to be on tv When he laughs it's kind of scary even on tv sometimes because it's not exactly real and it's not acting either. It's the laugh of somebody crazy mad, the kind of mad that takes weeks, months, a life to build, so the guy's almost shaking with it, with trying to cover it up, give him an edge when the opening comes. Seen it before, you can see it in the eyes like there's spoons pressed from behind and in the face muscles too, stretched tight to pack it all down just a little bit longer. This man's going to explode, he's set to go for it, you know it, you almost want to hunch your shoulder up, and you hope it'll happen sooner than later but hopefully when you're not around.

The only thing that *was* straight acting in the movie was the fights, so that was no help.

Didn't have any butter on my popcorn again, just Molly McButter and diet pop of course. Lost eleven pounds altogether.

Jamie's eye is yellow hideous and Wilf says people will think we've been beating him up.

Mon. 9th

Wilf says there's more layoff talk but there's always talk so what's the point in worrying.

Couldn't sleep last night. Dormez-vous? Dormez-vous? the words running through my head as though to make fun of me. The job's getting to me, definitely.

Told Wilf about the others thinking something's going to happen and all the cuts from the Correspondence/Visitors list, a sure sign. He just says watch yourself, like we're partners on a cop show or something, not really worried. Dad and both his parents think it's crazy my working there, worry all the time they say. But none of them knows what it's really like.

Course if Wilf is laid off we'll need the job.

Mar. 11

Kroger's back in today but Nancy's off sick. So I stop doing his work and start doing hers. It's like a conspiracy.

Lots of tension at work, an inmate got stabbed last night.

Ven would like to strip search us all for real, you get that feeling. Course he's got his orders and the metal detector's been acting up, the repairman was there when I went by.

Inmate Vogel says to me — Please Mrs. Gertz, will you read this? And he gives it to me, a poem. Here it is

> You brighten my days Mrs. Gertz
> When you leave for the day it sure hurts
> To know I won't see you or hear
> From any but inmates the guards and the queers
> Until you come back

First four lines is right anyway, I left it at work and it goes on for a page. Vogel took Cormier's place sweeping the outside office, always says hi, how's the weather. You're not supposed to encourage them or tell anything personal especially about your family, where you live.

He gave me the poem two days ago. But he wasn't at work today, deserted feeling in the halls just like the few days after Eddie Cormier got killed, you can't help but think. There's been dozens didn't show for work the last day or two. Sure sign of trouble. Something's up, everybody says.

Mar. 15

It's late at night and I feel stupid. Haven't been sleeping, been on edge, feel feverish but no temperature. Naturally thought it was just work, worrying about Wilf's job, Jamie fighting. Didn't even think about the diet pills which are basically speed. Which I *should* have known. Work in a prison after all.

Tomorrow I stop. Lost 16 pounds so far but it's not worth it. Wilf used to joke that an aspirin could knock me out, a Gravol pill really would, and I always have to tell doc-

Realemon

tors I'm oversensitive if it's painkillers, anything like that. Didn't even think to mention it with the diet pills. Probably too embarrassed to think of it.

Just have to keep on the diet without the pills.

I know it's the pills, it must be.

Mar. 16

Felt depressed all day, that song running through my head.

Mar. 20

Wilf just phoned from the tavern to say he got his pink slip. Said he'd be late celebrating his new-found freedom with the rest that got it. Watching hockey on the big screen.

I've gained back five pounds.

Ding dong ding.

$S\underline{tag}$

I was staring into the dusty glass of a framed Group of Seven print, wondering what would happen if I turned my neat schoolteacher's beard into a beatnik's goatee, when the phone rang.

I let it ring, scruffing up chin feathers, pressing palms over cheeks, dodging jackpines. Of course, to get the true Beat effect, I'd have to cut my hair shorter. In a box in the hall closet were shoes dating back a decade and no doubt there'd be some suitably hardworn sandals in that. Sunglasses — would that be right? — and, yes, a black cotton turtleneck from Army and Navy, run through the durable wash cycle three or four times. Perhaps I could even work up a talk on 1950s American counter-culture for my grade seven History class. We were on the fourth voyage with Radisson and Groseilliers just now, a trip I'd made many times, but with a little creative ...

"Hello?"

"Jesus, Burt. I almost gave up. What were you, in the can?"

"I was downstairs — washing my turtle on durable."

"Ya, well. I phoned your school. They said you went home sick."

"They have me confused with Groseilliers. It was he who fell ill at the head of the mighty Mississip. Pierre Esprit had to carry him on a travois."

Stag

"Right. Anyway, it's about the stag."

The person on the phone was Bruce Folks, one of my oldest friends. Bruce, training to be a nurse when I first met him in university, was now a hospital administrator; his housemate, Celia, was an engineer. The two had lived together for better than nine years and were about to tie the knot.

"What about it, Bruce?"

"Well, Celia and I were talking."

This meant trouble. Celia is one of those sad, rare birds whose imaginative faculty is completely missing — not just low, but absent, as good as pricked out by the lobotomist's needle. Not her fault of course, but endless problems for anyone near her: she tried to hide it, overcompensated wildly. Back in university was worst. Then, if any medium from a beer ad to an underground magazine labelled an activity adventurous, aesthetically in or merely right, Celia led the line to try it. New acquaintances of Celia invariably tended towards the eccentric, the artistic, the morally or politically extreme; at the first hint of a cause at all radical, off-base or sometimes just under-represented — you got it: there was Celia, loudly and dramatically espousing the party line. Of course, she was also the first to drop the new friend (a fraud, a fascist); denounce the cause (wrong-headed, irrelevant); or decry the experience as hollow (they all were, inevitably, to her). She simply didn't know. In the most basic terms, her interior gallery was missing that essential, constantly changing, not necessarily accurate self-portrait which the rest of us use as a standard when assigning worth to what the world offers. Celia was constitutionally unable to imagine, first and foremost, herself.

Fortunately, she'd calmed down a lot since the broken bones (sky-diving, of course) and weekend insurrections (animal rights, New Objectivism, midwifery) of school days; since the post-graduate year when she'd hauled Bruce off to do Development Aid work in Africa and landed them amidst a civil war; was calmer even since I'd linked up with them again in this province so far away from the one we'd all been brought up in. In a Celia-esque way, she'd become, almost, domestic. *Un*fortunately, she'd also recently cottoned on to the fact that I knew her secret and I'd been forced to . . . well, more on that later.

"What were you talking about, Bruce?"

"Well, we were thinking. You know, it *was* Celia's idea to begin with — that we have the stag."

I knew. The wedding was also Celia's idea. As was living together instead of getting married. In a complicated way not worth untangling, getting married now that it no longer mattered was by way of self-punishment for Celia's really wanting to be married in the first place.

"And you were thinking?"

"Yes. Well." Bruce took a deep breath here. "Well, we were thinking that it would be nice if instead of the cards and beer in the private room at Flanigan's, it would be a nice reversal of roles if maybe we *guys* stayed at home tonight, ate cake, had door prizes, played games, you know more of a shower thing. When you think of it, it *could* be okay, no reason why we absolutely *have* to get drunk to have fun, Celia says *she's* been forced to sit through *dozens* of these things *lots* of times over the last . . ."

It was cruel to have let him go even this long — Kamikaze Rhetoric we used to call it when Bruce-the-Reasonable was forced into explicating a Celia-ism, Emfastic Mode; unchecked, the results were not a pretty sight — but I couldn't submit without some protest.

"Bruce, before it was all we could do to get out of having stag movies."

"I know, I know, but hear me out. She and some of her women friends are of course going to a bar . . ."

Stag

"Why don't we *all* go to a bar? To Flanigan's. That'd be really iconoclastic."

"Well, they're going to see these male strippers, and after..."

"I don't care. Might be interesting to see a twelve inch wang. It's gotta be better than cake."

"I think the idea is that *men* along would be inhibiting..."

"Only if we were dressed. Perhaps..."

"And there is a certain amount of *atonement* involved. After all, women have had to go through this stuff for *decades*, more..."

"I think I've atoned enough, Bruce."

Although I hadn't meant to do it that way, and felt immediately guilty, that stopped him. I'd been a widower for about eighteen months, and at thirty-one this gave me a certain unique status among my friends. I wasn't set religiously against dining out on my position — I had, literally — but it was the type of credit that could easily get overdrawn before anyone, last of all yourself, realized it.

"Here's something different, Bruce," I said into the uncertain emptiness. If Bruce only knew it — I doubted he did — he was playing *me* right. I have an aversion to dead air. "Here's something. Why don't we get *Gordie* drunk tonight? Steal *his* clothes and dump *him* naked on the neighbour's lawn. Or better, on Celia's parents'. We'll figure out how to get him to southern Ontario later."

Bruce gave a relieved laugh, something like "heh-heh." I had an easy time imagining him among his fellow hospital administrators when he did that.

"Okay, Bruce. You're on. But — where are you right now?"

"At a health services administrators conference at the university. In fact, I have to run a session in about two minutes."

"Probably be the one redeeming thing that happens all day."

I was being sincere. In contrast to Celia, Bruce has a peculiar species of imagination that runs so deep he doesn't even know he has it. In dozens of small, innovative ways, he'd made the lives of people in pain just that much more tolerable in every hospital he'd ever worked in.

"Ah."

Bruce is also modest.

"Anyway, what I was saying is — first of all, I'm bringing a bottle. Whether you tell Celia or no is up to you."

He went along.

"And *I'd* better tell the rest of them. As best man . . . "

"Witness. Even Celia couldn't see her way clear to . . . "

"Witness, then. As best *witness*, I'm the one who should have been arranging this do from the start. If I leave it to you it'll end up just the two of us wolfing cake tonight."

"Okay. I'm late. Oh, I already cancelled Flanigan's, and Seal got some food, etcetera. See you later, then."

And that was that. I was by then sunk deep in the bowels of a sprung chair, nose to navel with twenty pounds of excess belly fat. Cake, indeed.

I didn't really want to, but the phone was by my side and it had to be done, so I picked up the book, flipped, then started dialling.

With one of Bruce's hospital administrator cronies, I was brisk and business-like. *The location of the Director's meeting has been changed*, I tried to put in my voice; *I have been seconded to the job of informing you. Circulate a memo to this effect among your staff*. It turned out the fellow I talked to couldn't make the stag no matter where, but he'd tell the rest in the office.

To the representative of the staff of male nurses and the larger group of male orderlies — Bruce liked to keep in touch with these people no matter what hospital he worked

Stag

in, though it was years since he'd been one of them — I was chummy, suggesting, without saying: stag movies, girls in cakes, high stakes poker with easy pickings to be gleaned from their bosses. The person I talked to would also spread the word, although personally his wife was pregnant, momentarily due, and he thought he might give it a miss.

With only one person was I honest.

"Celia," I told Gordie, when I got hold of him at the college. "The stag."

I described the situation.

"Damn," he said. "I was half looking forward to a good piss-up tonight too. Nobody's going to come now. If they do, they stay ten minutes to be polite and fuck off."

I was becoming of much the same opinion. The stag had been a late-breaking idea and Bruce had never invited as many people as he'd let on to Celia. Those who did come and didn't leave immediately would stay on purely out of embarrassment for Bruce. Not that that would bother him, but still, it wasn't much of a celebration.

"*You're* coming?" The thought had just occurred that even Gordie might jump ship.

"Ya. Fuck."

An alternate plan began to form and I offered it up to him.

"Ya. Okay. Lesser evil. Can't stand them admin types anyway. And that orderly crew — they're always so bloody placid. Comes from inserting suppositories all day. Ever notice? Their right index finger always has a sheen to it."

I told him I hadn't. Then, as an afterthought, I asked him if he knew any Beat poets. Gordie taught remedial English at the college, but between times he was a practising poet. I had six copies of a badly printed book of his to prove it.

"Ginsberg," he said immediately, tagging on an indrawn breath which suggested he was holding back a score of others he could tell me if he wanted. I was pretty sure he'd shot the bolt, but in the interests of friendship decided not to call him on it. I was fairly certain and it wasn't crucial.

"Know anything he wrote?" I asked doubtfully, as though it would be surprising indeed if anyone possessed such esoterica off the top of his head.

"'Howl'." Again the breath, again the suggestion that Gordie could rattle off the entire *oeuvre* of this Ginsberg if he felt like it.

"Thanks, Gordie. It's not important. Come here first and we'll walk over to Bruce's together."

Gordie hung up and I took a moment to wonder, as I had before, how long he would survive teaching my grade sevens. The answer, for a number of reasons, was always the same: not long.

I phoned the admin guy and told him the meeting was cancelled and to distribute a second memo to that effect. He agreed.

I phoned the orderly and told him we'd found out our stripper was a transvestite so we were postponing. He laughed politely, said he'd pass the word, and forgot to ask the real reason, or maybe didn't care. I tried to think of a tactful way of discovering if his index finger was sheened, couldn't, so ended by wishing his wife the best. He promised a cigar through Bruce.

Deed done, I recradled in the flabby upholstery to weigh the consequences of my actions.

The idea was that, if we three *had* to partake in this hybrid ritual — eating cake; becoming by slow degrees boozily nostalgic, boozily philosophic, even boozily silent; pretending later to have played games — it was better to do it alone than self-consciously under the embarrassed eyes of, at most, three or four strangers. Gordie too had been part of the inner circle in university years, our reunion in this distant prairie city only partly accident. Alone, together, we might even wring some incidental significance from the gathering.

Stag

The only flaw in the plan was Celia.

Celia, predictable in her unpredictableness, would be one of two things: a) pleased at what could be construed as well-meaning impulsiveness; or, b) angry that her unorthodoxy, if that was a word, had been foiled. There was a final possibility, that c) she'd be both these things, if she had the energy, because she admired violent mood swings as the mark of the creative personality.

Weighing, I decided that Celia could go fuck herself.

That out of the way, I managed a violent swing of my own, and was standing once again before the picture. Formally presented by Bruce and Celia one memorable May day at the end of our first shared year of university, the thing had caused great anguish to Celia, who'd fairly constantly considered the Group intolerably bourgeois ever since. A wedding gift. For just a few seconds I allowed myself to penetrate the glassy surface: scrambling over rock; darting; sucking in my gut to hide behind one thin tree after another — all in a moment, one man hide-and-seek.

I walked to the washroom and started up the electric razor — skipping past the comforting hum of shaving gear directly to the this-means-business rattle of the sideburn trimmer. I hacked away at my face, making a mess, till I had sideburns and cheek hairs dispatched. I did more work under my chin and along the throat line. Retreating from the machine age, I used a safety razor on all newly naked skin. I ended with a goatee alright, but with my longish hair it wasn't quite the effect I was aiming for. I now had a slightly Teutonic appearance, a sort of Beethoven, recently moved into psychiatry.

One problem was that the goatee was simply too short and neat. To remedy this, I got out a pair of scissors and nipped away randomly to spike it up. Moving to the hair, I formed a two-inch ponytail with thumb and forefinger and cut it off — the ponytail, that is. The notion of somehow transferring this newly unattached hair to my chin occurred, but when I tried it on for size in the mirror, my face got serious and I told myself to shape up. I did some more cutting up top, trimming, thinning, and flattening out what remained with baby oil, then tousling that up. I'd taken on a slightly demonic look, which I judged to be close enough.

I entered the bedroom and without much searching turned up a pair of straight-leg blue jeans. Straight-legs were either in or out of fashion again, I couldn't remember. These had a mucusy streak of something stuck on one leg, which from a distance could pass for one of several bodily fluids, a touch which seemed appropriate. I put them on.

I didn't have time for the Army and Navy, let alone for running a turtleneck through durable wash even once. It struck me though that the reason I'd first thought of a turtle was I'd seen one somewhere around. I went through several drawers before I opened one containing some of Alice's old things. The drawer was about the only place Celia'd overlooked when going through the closets and bathroom cabinets — clearing away, she'd told me with Glad bags in her belt and a tear in her eye, the old memories. Grief has nothing to do with imagination, I'd have known that even if Celia hadn't offered proof.

Alice's shirt offered no memories — I couldn't remember her ever wearing it. I was standing before a full-length mirror when I put it on, and the neck unrolled to cover my face, the way turtlenecks do. For a moment I left it that way. I wondered if I looked like a cartoon character I remembered who wore his turtleneck like that, up over his face. The character, nameless to me now, used to figure on the tiny squares of wax paper which came with penny bubblegum. I wished I could see myself. I wondered how he saw. I wished I had someone here who could see me and tell me what I looked like.

I stopped wishing, pulled the collar down and the sleeves

up, since they were far too short. Not bad, really. The throat was a little tight, but my hair had got tousled a degree or two closer to the beatnik ideal. I put on a pair of blue-tinted sunglasses I had also found in the drawer.

The final thing, of course, was the sandals. I had to perform a sort of archaeological dig through the hall closet box to find these, each level representing a different epoch of civilization. There were a great number of Alice's shoes, the shoe box being the one thing I wouldn't let Celia touch — not through any secret desire to enshrine Alice's cast-off joggers, I'd claimed at the time, but because Celia, with the best of intentions, might accidentally throw out some perfectly good platforms, say, or a pair of oxfords with solid miles still ahead of them; fashions change, I'd told her gnomically. Eventually, I found the sandals — the classic Indian kind, molded and burnished by a thousand summer wearings — and I was set.

I returned to the living-room and searched out an anthology of verse I vaguely knew to be collecting dust somewhere in the bookcases. I looked up Ginsberg and found what I wanted. "Howl" was also there and I recognized the first lines, must have heard it read somewhere. The poem kept me going till Gordie rang from downstairs, then appeared at my door: skinny, tall, with his miser's six-pack under his arm and a slight twist of preoccupation on his face, his usual expression. He gave me and my get-up the once over, but apparently found nothing worthy of comment. I'd meant to bring his book along, as a prop sort of, but that decided me against it. I brought the anthology instead, and a full bottle of Scotch.

Bruce and Celia's house is three blocks from the apartment building I live in, so Gordie and I didn't have much time for talk on the way. In the cool of the October night, I gave him a second chance to respond properly to my beatnik costume, explaining about grade seven classes and counter-culture, but he really wasn't interested. Gordie, I always forget, is both experienced and naive in different ways from other people. Having lived his life among poets — his mother was one, for God's sake, and English Departments breed them like maggots — he tends to be blasé about deviancy in any form, particularly dress, in poets this usually being attributable to the "shtick" and in Gordie's experience most people being poets. On the other hand, such rarefied living has somehow left him with the idea that beneath the shtick we're all basically the same (like him, in other words). If someone were to propose, for instance, that the problems of natives could be simply solved by sterilization at birth — an idea seriously bandied by a pair of gems in the teachers' lounge recently — Gordie was capable of mulling for hours, trying to invent the punchline, thinking it must be an off-colour joke. I'd long ago decided that anyone that intrinsically optimistic couldn't be all bad.

When we arrived at Bruce's we found that Celia had already gone. Bruce, out of his suit and into jeans and a flannel shirt, was once again the Bruce I had gone to school with. He relieved us of our parcels, directed our jackets to the hall wall-pegs with a glance, and led the way downstairs to the basement, an area I was already familiar with from helping him build some partitions. While he stashed Gordie's beer in the rec room fridge — there were already a few dozen in there, more Celia sabotage — I explained about the change in the guest list.

"Oh," he said. He didn't seem overly disappointed on his own behalf — Bruce had never been big on parties, though he had tried over the years — but seemed afraid somebody's feelings might be hurt. I explained about expectant babies and prior commitments, trying to hint that it wouldn't be too great a hardship for the guests to give the festivities a miss, while at the same time not suggest that probably nobody really wanted to come anyway.

We got drinks going and Bruce, always dependable, asked about my costume and new face. He thought it might have something to do with Hallowe'en coming up, an explanation I hadn't considered, so I told him yes, that was partly it, but it was mostly for the kids.

This struck a chord. I have a largely unearned reputation among a select few for being a dedicated and innovative teacher. Partly this comes from the fact that I take my young scholars on as many field trips as I can get away with, often subsidizing them out of my own pocket. I've never lied about the reason for this — I hate being cooped up in the classroom as much as the kids do — but the Few have never believed me. The rest of the rep is based on my costume sessions, the most notable of which occurred the day I came dressed as a *coureur de bois*, complete with colourful waist-cinch and thirty smaller cinches for my students. The cinches, an historical fact, were never intended as charming ethnic garb, but rather were used to bind up hernias gained from lives of carrying heavy loads. I'd asked my stomach-bound class to imagine the weighty burdens, imagine the hernias, and inevitably had gone into great biological detail on the subject, hernias being central to the issue and seventh-graders notoriously shaky on anatomy. Naturally, word got out that I was not only departing from the curriculum but was conducting sex education classes, and this had led to the most public in a series of clashes with the administration — which in themselves tended to confirm my status among the Few, administrators (excepting Bruce) never having been too popular among them.

Bruce was keen to hear details of this latest experiment in classroom theatre. He couldn't quite see — although he genuinely wanted to discover — how I was going to fit in fifties counter-culture with the early North American explorers. Many people would find it odd that a childless male nurse-cum-hospital paper-pusher would know the approximate course outline of a grade school history class, but I didn't and should have known better.

I changed the topic, turned up the stereo, and busied myself recharging drinks. We talked desultorily for a while about teaching remedial English, the poor remuneration thereof, and the usefulness of so-called professional conferences. When the conversation seemed ripe for return to grade seven classes and the Beat movement, I suggested Bruce take us on a tour of the house to show us his latest improvements.

Bruce was always willing to do this, though never boring about it. An expert, entirely self-taught cabinet-maker, you couldn't help but think he'd missed his calling. The most recent proof lay upstairs, in some bookcases built into an impossibly out-of-square corner of Celia's study. He also showed us some hand-turned trim he'd been installing on the inner (the inner, mind you) doorframes of some closets, and described the newest developments in plans for the kitchen cabinets he'd been building in his mind for months.

When we detoured to the basement to view some newly purchased and highly esoteric tools at his work table, I was able to identify the mucusy stuff on my straight-legged pants: a special kind of glue, acquired when I helped him build the partitions some months ago.

The tour was interrupted several times for freshening of drinks and changing of records — the entire house reverberating with Beatles and Creedence Clearwater Revival and Three Dog Night, sometimes basement and upstairs turntables going at the same time, sometimes kitchen liquor supplies raided when the basement ones seemed too far away. Somehow the house tour stretched out over an hour, Bruce suddenly remembering he had a cedar chest upstairs he hadn't shown us, Gordie reminded of some record he thought he'd once heard *chez* Bruce and us all going through piles to find it, me recollecting the African mask I'd been meaning to borrow and it turning out to be not in the attic but in the spare bedroom after all. We were like three wise men, unsure of their star.

Finally, though, we settled down to reminiscing about the old days — our old plans, dreams, emotions; Alice's name gingerly touched on once or twice. Submerging deeper into my beatnik role, I began inserting more and more "heps" and "cats" and "daddy-o's" into my speech, and finally ended by declaiming "Howl" for a few stanzas, Gordie criticizing my rendering and taking over in his breathless reading style which you were always sure you'd heard somewhere before but weren't sure where. From this he moved to one of his own poems-in-progress, revising as he went, with great pause for creative breath.

Somehow the time passed in the bottom of the empty house, and I think we all would have declared it a successful stag at one a.m. — when we were half-way through singing "Eli's Coming" for the third time, almost in harmony — which was when Celia walked in. You could tell someone must have decided for her that male stripping wasn't really a viable art form and that watching it wasn't truly adventurous. You could also tell she was looking for a fight.

"You guys are disgusting," she projected, three stair steps above our heads.

"'Never get away, never get away, from the fear and the heartache,'" I told her, solo.

"You most of all. I suppose you're responsible. What have you done to your face? You look like something the dog dragged in."

There had been a price to pay for letting Celia know I knew her secret. A once friendly, bantering relationship had changed, on Celia's part, to something much nastier. Increasingly she meant violence — was out either to punish me or goad me into blowing her cover, I wasn't sure which — and neither of us had the brains to stay away.

"— spired impulse . . . " I started and couldn't continue. Something was wrong. Usually I shrugged her off, jollied her past it. But my mouth, empty of lyrics, wasn't working, didn't want to work. There was a weird internal torquing sensation, a wrenching of diaphragm part voluntary, part not, hard to explain, not just the drinks.

"What?"

My voice was still defunct, but I managed to knock over a glass of Scotch, as though to illustrate.

"Idiot!"

"Seal." This from Bruce.

"That's the rug we brought all the way back from Central Africa. That old man from the settlement north of . . . "

Something ripped. I could almost hear it, inside, like coarse fabric giving way. Whatever it was had been stretching, tautening all day, maybe longer. The drinks had only fooled me into thinking that the tension had relaxed.

Call it inspired impulsiveness or something else, but my fingers toyed with one of the darts displayed suggestively on a sidetable next to me, and it was not with the intention of playing party games that I picked it up. I could still feel the stiff burlapy ends fluttering in my gut. Anatomy-book hernias and brightly coloured sashes passed through my mind as I let the missile fly, aiming roughly at a row of bric-a-brac shelved behind the finely finished bar. It didn't stick in anything, but did knock over a large carved animal, one of the things Bruce and Celia had brought back with them from Africa.

Celia shrieked. Really. She rushed to the bar, disappeared behind it, and re-emerged cradling the figure in her hands as though it were a wounded child.

Stag

"The one truly good piece of Art we have in the house," she said, as though to herself, as though struggling to believe the tragedy had really taken place. As though she knew. As though she had a right to be present at all at the moment, which she didn't. The reason she thought the piece good was because I'd told her — which it was, in a way, not bad at all, considering.

In the meantime, Gordie had decided the party was over and had begun to edge toward the stairs. I stood too. Celia watched all three of us, speechless. This was a rare condition for Celia, as good a moment as any to leave, so with a parting nod to Bruce we started to. Not fast enough, though.

Before we reached the first step, Celia, ostensibly addressing Bruce, was saying:

"How much longer do we have to coddle him? She's been dead a year and a half now."

It was a classic scene: the dagger thrown at the exposed back, but missing to stick in the doorpost. The handle still vibrated as I pulled it out.

"Don't worry, Seal," I flicked over my shoulder, words powerful in my mouth once more, three steps above *her* now. "Don't worry. Next time the UNICEF show's in town I'll buy you three of 'em."

"Don't be stupid. This is unique. Handcarved..."

"Ebony Impala. $12.95 Canadian. Cheaper by the..."

"...that artisan in the village where we..."

But you could hear the doubt creeping into her voice; and before I reached the top of the stairs I was feeling sorry for her. Poor Celia. Who did she have now to tell her that it's all an adventure, that nothing's original, least of all the pain and next least our little squirmings to make it less? Who would tell her that the very unoriginality of hurt, the sharedness of it, was sometimes the only comfort left?

Poor Seal, I thought, hitching my belt into the night like a drunken sailor. Why wasn't that knowledge the signature on her portrait, the way it was for almost everyone else in the world?

Before we'd walked a block, Gordie's gaze had fixed on our feet, particularly mine, the more conspicuous with bare heels dragging concrete and sandals six sizes too small.

"'Who killed the pork chops?'" he suddenly said; then: "'What price bananas? Are you my angel?' — *That's* Ginsberg."

He said this last in a tone as though I might argue. I didn't. They were the only lines of poetry Alice had ever memorized. She'd quoted them often to us, revelling in the out-of-context absurdity; and sometimes, to me, just whispered them, just revelling.

It took Gordie perhaps another block before he digested the silence, before he pulled from his pocket the swiped heel of my bottle of Scotch, and before he offered a toast to prove that even minor poets can sometimes find the right words.

"To Alice," he said, swigging and passing the bottle.

*L*andlock

Lately, after school, I've been going downtown in the car with my mom, if she's got any shopping to do. Sometimes, depending on her mood and depending if the weather's good, she'll let me drive home. On the backroads. Seven tenths of a mile is all it is, right on, by the odometer. Blackmail really too, for just that little ways I don't even get to drive every time anyways. All it is she wants is just somebody to keep her company and to carry out groceries when she's done shopping. It's illegal though, me driving, because I'm not sixteen yet. On June 21, that's when I will be. It's just that I want to get my licence right away after my birthday, without fooling around forever with my Beginner's.

I guess I don't mind all that much, going with my mom. There's nothing much to do at home anyways but watch the four-thirty movie. What I don't know is why she has to come *here* all the time, to the IGA, right in the middle of town like it is, with everybody likely to be hanging around. Not that I care what any of those guys think. It's just that, well, you don't need everybody seeing you out shopping with your mom like it was the great thrill of your life or something, or seeing you waiting around out here in the parking lot, even. Not if you're a guy. She's pretty good about it though. When she's finished in the store she comes out and gives me a wave, so I know it's time to come in and carry out the groceries. Or if there's only a few things, she'll carry them out herself.

Still, like I say, I don't much like being around here out in the open. So I end up like now, slouching down in the seat kind of, leaning over a bit, and hanging on to something — this old roadmap — like I was just bent down to get it. The roadmap's just in case somebody does walk by and happens to see me down here.

It's sort of slushy in here today, what with the snow we've been getting lately. There's puddles on the floor and it smells like old rubber and cigarette ashes, even though nobody in the family smokes. Except me sometimes, but that's only at noon hour outside the high school.

It's still winter out now, it being only the end of March. But it's been warming right up, and even when it does snow, like today, it's been coming down soft and sticky, and turning all to grey mush soon as it hits the pavement. It's the kind of snow we used to make iceballs out of back in grade school — it'd melt down easy and get hard fast. Just lobbing one of those suckers even, it was enough to dent a car or break a window. If you got hit by one, it'd leave a bruise — a big round sucker — for weeks. But nobody ever did, get hit that is, back when we used to make them. It was part of the rules. You could throw ordinary snowballs and wash people's faces. And you'd wrestle, and sometimes even get into a fight. But hardly nobody ever got hit by an iceball, or even a snowball with a rock in it.

Jesus though, it's getting cold out here. But today's Thursday, the big shopping day. So she'll be in there a while yet, I know.

You know, it wouldn't bother me so much, going in the store there just to get warmed up a bit, except for, well, except for Mr. Legget being in there, I guess. Old Mr. Legget, my grade eight teacher a couple years ago who quit before the year was over. I guess he wasn't really old. Young really. But weird. It's funny too, I never think of him much except for like now, when I'm close to the store. And it's not that I'm even likely going to see him if I do go in. And when I do — I mean when I have other times, seen him — mostly he'll be way in the back of the store, in the produce section, not even near the check-out at the front, and kind of turned sideways away from me. Maybe humming to himself. Or at least it will seem like that, like he's humming — you can't really tell, him being so far away. I never really look at him myself, just kind of out the side of my eye, him there stacking grapefruits into a pyramid maybe, or lining up lettuces in cellophane wrap like they was rows of students in a classroom or something. All the time with one of those white jackets on, like doctors or dentists wear. It's not that I'm afraid he'll see me even, you know, there in a grocery store, like I'm shopping. It's just that, well, that I'd rather *I* didn't have to see him. Or just that we didn't have to be in a place where we might see each other. Oh I don't know what I mean. I mean he might not even recognize me, after two years. He looked towards me once, almost straight at me, and didn't even seem to know me.

Jesus, I wish I'd stayed at home and watched the four-thirty movie or something. Or that I could have went out hunting with the guys after school like we used to. I wish Mom would hurry up with those groceries. You know, before too, he'd do the same damn thing. Wear the same damn jacket every day. Purple corduroy it was, with thick cords and wide spaces in between. And sometimes do that thing with his arms, crossing them in front of him, and sticking out his elbows so his bare arms would be showing there in front of him, like a hairy white "X."

And the humming too. Some people will tell you he never started that until near the end. But it's not true. Right from the first he'd be humming when us kids had in-class work to do or he was up at the blackboard writing. Soft then, but the first week even. I remember because somebody asked what it was he was humming, as a joke kind of. And him stopping and crossing up his arms real hard the way he would sometimes. It was a sea shanty, he said, but he'd forgot the title.

Mostly this was just in the first term of grade eight when he was doing all this. Stuff like sitting up on the edge of his desk — doing that about a hundred times a day by the end, just hopping up there for a minute, fidgeting and rocking, resting I guess, and getting ready to take off again. Or the walking too fast, down the sides of the room or up at the blackboard, asking questions that nobody would hear and he'd answer himself, waving his arms all the while, his jacket flapping. He was a pretty small guy with kind of a long face and he'd look like some crazy purple bird. Or sometimes he'd be showing us things — pictures in books that you couldn't see anyways from the back of the room, or different kinds of rocks and minerals, or scientific toys like that one thing made of shiny metal balls on strings that got stole. And we didn't even have him for Science.

And talking. If he wasn't talking for a second he'd be humming, even in between sentences. But mostly it would be talking, always a bit too fast so that mostly you wouldn't even bother trying to keep up, and going from bad to worse as the term went by. Except the few times when he was doing that thing with his arms, leaning forward and his wrists crossed up like they'd be. Then, sometimes, you'd hear. It was like he just had a few things that he had to get said before he took off again, and they'd be short and somehow you could hear them better. It's funny, but I still remember some of the things he said when he did that. They never seemed to have much to do with what he was teaching. Like one day it was real foggy out and he was saying about cod fishing off the Grand Banks of Newfoundland. Kind of interesting, except we were supposed to be talking about Africa. Or another time he said we should start a students' council. He said that we really should, that other schools had them, and he'd help us with it if we wanted. He said some other stuff about it, and that we should see him after class if we wanted to. It sounded like a pretty good idea at the time, like a few of the other ideas he'd had before. But then it would be the same as before. He'd be off and moving again, waving his arms, and his voice just a voice that you didn't pay much attention to. Billy Waters would make one of his faces, Fats would burp, and Gear Nob would roll his eyes just a little so you knew there wasn't any doubts about it — this guy was a real asshole. And it was true too, at least when he was moving around.

I remember now I had a theory about all that moving. It's stupid really. But sitting back there, watching him talk Math or Geography or whatever while he moved around, I thought he was like one of those guys in the movies, that if he stopped moving, if he sat still too long, maybe something bad would happen. And that thing when he crossed his arms, that was like when you see the hero warding off vampires or something. That's what it looked like from the back of the room anyways. Pretty stupid, I know. I'm always thinking of stupid stuff like that, just because there's nothing much else to do.

Like I say, this was all back in the fall term of grade eight. Before January when he really went nuts giving out the strap — he'd never give it himself before that, which was another weird thing about him. Not that nobody ever got the strap before January. Even with Mr. Legget there was only so much you could get away with before getting sent to the principal for him to give it. And no matter what anybody will tell you, nobody was any too eager to get strapped.

So that's why I ended up spending a lot of time just kind of being there, filling up space — just sitting at my desk trying not to think how itchy my bum was from getting wet in the school yard, and keeping one eye on what was going on around me with the other kids. You had to keep your eyes open, just for your own safety, just in case there was, say, a rubber fight brewing or something — if you didn't you were likely to find the side of your head plastered with the chewed up rubbers we all used to shoot out of hollow pens. Just trying to keep my mind occupied, really, is all I was trying to do. And since he'd be up there anyways, a lot of the time, teetering there on the edge of his desk or doing some other thing to attract our attention, naturally I'd look at him. I don't know, maybe I was just more bored that year.

It didn't start out that way though, being bored. It was a good fall that year, back in September. It seems a long time ago now somehow. It was still like summer out then. This was back before they filled in Hutch's Pond out down the plug tracks, and there were still lots of frogs out around there. It was still warm enough to even go skinny dipping out at the Brickyard Pond, out past the other end of town. There were still lots of birds to shoot since they hadn't migrated yet. We'd take our pellet guns and go out hunting just about every day after school, even though we'd hardly get anything with so many guys crashing around all together. Mostly we were just busy kind of being around outside and getting to know one another again, even though most of us, at least those who lived in town and didn't have farms they had to help out on, had seen each other off and on all summer. But it was the first time really, since the year before, that we were all back together in one big bunch.

It wasn't even too bad at school then. It was all still kind of new to us being the oldest guys in the school and none of the bigger guys to give us shit. So I guess we all felt kind of big ourselves. Anyways, we spent a lot of time sort of testing each other out, when we weren't in class. Deciding who was okay, and who wasn't. Even though most of that was taken

Landlock

care of back in grade seven or even earlier. I guess it was then though that I really got on the inside, back at the beginning of grade eight. Even though I was okay even before that.

It was one thing that happened out hunting at Hutch's Pond, right off, in the beginning of September, the thing that got me in. Nothing really. An accident. We were hunting, a bunch of us, maybe seven or eight — Fats and Billy Waters and Gordie Percy and I don't remember who else. And Gear Nob. He was the toughest guy in the school, before grade eight even, from fighting all the bigger guys, guys a lot bigger than he was. He was pretty small, you'd be surprised — lots of guys were who didn't know any better. Anyways, he was there, right in front of me, because we were walking single file along one of the paths, through the marshy bush part, right next to the Pond. I was the last in line. It was kind of dark out, I remember, even though it was pretty well right after school. With all of us tramping around, any birds or frogs that were out took off before we got anywhere near enough for a decent shot. The only birds you'd even see mostly would be flying way off in front of us or to the side. Once in a while one would land in one of the trees off in the swampy part away from the path, but it'd still be way out of range for a pellet gun. Everybody was just about ready to call it quits for the day, you could tell just from the way they were walking, when I saw a bird, a starling it was, land in one of the trees way off to the side of us and just sit there bouncing up and down on the top branch. It was out of range like others we'd walked right by, but I figured I might as well take a shot at it since I knew we'd be going home soon anyways. So I did. And it dropped, straight down, not even a flutter. It was hard to believe, a terrific shot, and I felt great about it. For about a second. Then I realized without even looking over that nobody had even stopped, nobody had seen and there was no way you were going to go splashing up to your waist in swamp water to find a dead bird. I was deciding whether or not to even mention it. This was all like in a second, half a second. But I didn't get to decide because there was Gear Nob, looking right at me, and the next minute telling everybody what a great shot I was, and how he would never have believed it, the shot I made. It was twice as good than if everybody else had seen it, like it was something just between the two of us. Later, about a week and a half after that, somebody tried to pick a fight with me — Larry Lachance who had only been at the school going on his second year, and who really wasn't on the inside even though he played ground hockey with us at recess and noon hour. Gear Nob was standing around at the time and the guy and me were just kind of pushing each other around — you know, where you're not exactly sure whether you're playing around or not, but you're pretty sure you're not. Gear Nob just said to the guy, kind of casual, that he wouldn't like to be in anybody's shoes if they got in a fight with me. And this Larry backed off. After that, after what Gear Nob said, I probably would have beat him anyways.

It's hard to believe about Gear Nob. He got that job at the car factory in the city just a couple of months ago. And then he got nailed for stealing a car.

Gear Nob. It's a weird name, when you think about it. Funny.

This wasn't what I was talking about anyways. I was talking about the way it was back at the beginning of the year, back in grade eight, with all of us just kind of testing each other out. What I meant was just that I was kind of lucky not having to get in fights all the time, and not having to do any of the really crazy stuff on Hallowe'en night — like Larry Lachance having to dump that box of shit on the cop shop steps, or Gordie Percy pouring gasoline over the plastic flamingo on somebody's lawn and lighting it — you know, stuff that scares you to do, but in a bad way, not just a little bit like ordinary Hallowe'en stuff. Maybe that's why I could notice other things more, because I didn't have to worry about doing that crazy stuff all the time.

Like back in early fall when all this was going on, you could tell Mr. Legget was kind of testing us too — you know, seeing how far he could go, him being new to the school and all. And naturally, we'd be doing the same thing back to him — taking it slow, to see how much we could get away with.

It was because of that — because of everybody taking it slow, and because of what I said before about us guys being mostly busy outside — that most of us didn't really notice how weird he was, more than any other teacher we'd ever had. I mean, there were lots of little things that he'd been doing right from the beginning, but somehow didn't really bother us then. Like he'd let us get up any time we wanted to sharpen our pencils, without even asking. That didn't bother us — it was great. And it didn't bother us either that he'd underline his titles in coloured chalk on the blackboard, or that the titles were a little bit weird. Not at first. It wasn't till November that we started to get real bored, what with it getting dark out earlier and earlier, and there being not so many birds out, a lot of them having flown south. It wasn't till then that we started to notice.

But the thing was, it was like we were too late or something — like since we'd been letting him get away with it so much, there wasn't any way he was going to stop. In fact, it seemed like the more we acted up, the worse he got. Like he'd be rocking on his desk even more, and moving faster and faster when he was walking around. And his arms, like he was treading water. There got to be extra underlinings in different colours under his weird titles. And it seemed like with all the colour gone from outside, now that the leaves were down and we were into winter, his jacket somehow got to be more purple. It was strange.

Jesus, I don't know why I keep thinking about this guy. I

mean, I don't even care about him. And it sounds like I'm really cutting him down. I don't mean to. He wasn't bad. He asked me to stay behind a couple of times, to clean boards or something, and it wasn't like he wanted me to work or something. It was just like he was trying to be friendly. Of course I never did. I don't know. It seems a long time ago, back in grade eight. I'm in ten now. It's just because I'm sitting here, you know, knowing he's in the store there, and knowing I'm liable to run into him sooner or later, having to go in there like I do. And knowing too that I'm not even going to get to drive home, what with all the shitty weather we've been getting. I guess mostly it's just that I'm bored though. There just doesn't seem much to do what with this town way out in the sticks the way it is and me not even having a chance to get my licence till summer. And what with most of the guys I used to hang around with not even in my classes.

Like for one thing, he wasn't even from around here. This is a small town, even if it is near the city, and most teachers, you'd know their families, or somebody's parents would know their family, or even if they came from the city, somebody would know somebody who knew them. But he came from out east, from the Maritimes somewheres. Went to a teacher's school there, I guess. Even taught there for a few years before coming here. Somebody's dad or something was on the school board and it got passed on. Maybe that's where he got a lot of his weird ideas from. Although I heard another rumour, after he quit, that they weren't too crazy about him out there either. All I know is that he wasn't like the rest of the teachers, not even Miss Feldon, our Art teacher in grade seven, who had to leave.

There were lots of things he did, but somehow, like I was saying, it was the little things he'd been doing right from the beginning and just got a little worse that got to you most. Like I said about the underlining. And the titles too. They were always a little funny, but they got worse. Things like

Landlock

"That Old Man Crazy Lazy River" when we were talking about the Mississippi River, or the Amazon, or whatever it was; or, "The Last of the Red Hot Ice Cold Glaciers" when we were talking about the Ice Age.

And other things too. From the beginning he'd say stuff like "sing me a song" when somebody was saying something and they were on the right track. Or, "wowfineandrighton," all run together like that. Sometimes, first thing in the morning when nobody felt like it, it would be "Har me buckos," like we were playing pirates or something. And other stuff, more all the time, like he was collecting it. I counted how many times he said stuff like that, just in one afternoon once, just to prove how . . . well, how stupid he was. Twenty-four times. Plus the titles. I wrote it down, you know, each time he'd say stuff and the time alongside it. Like I was a secret agent or something. I was going to show the guys but I didn't. I was even thinking I might show it to him, but naturally I didn't. I don't even know why I did it myself. I think I was just mad or something, like he was making fun of us or something. I think I just wanted him to stop it, and act a little more normal.

Anyways, there's no doubt we started acting up more, it happened that way every year, and the teachers, they just kind of expected it, as far as I could tell.

It was one time after we'd been really bad that the thing with the desks getting moved around happened. It was around about one of the last days of November, after we'd been really noisy for a couple of days running, even the girls, worse than we'd ever been in any class. It was during a big rubber fight. There were three or four guys lined up at the pencil sharpener shooting rubbers at the rest of us, and us shooting back. Mr. Legget was up at the board at the time, writing some long lesson and humming especially hard the way he would when we were acting up and he didn't want to hear. The thing was, the guys at the sharpener had the vantage point and good big mouthfuls of rubber and the rest of us were taking a beating. So we started groaning real loud when we got hit and yelling for each other to look out, a few of us even ducking under our desks to get out of the way — trying to catch Mr. Legget's attention so he'd turn around and we could get a breather. For a while he just hummed harder. Then finally — he might even have got hit himself — he came and took about half a dozen hollow pens away from different guys. That straightened everybody up for a while, at least till he was done the lesson. Afterwards he said we were going to move the desks around. We thought he just meant he was going to make the worst of us sit up at the front, like it happened in other classes, so he could keep an eye on us. But he did a funny thing — he made us write out on a piece of paper the names of two people we'd like to sit next to and two others who were the second choice. This was before lunch hour. After lunch, when we came back, he made us push all our desks around in groups of three. Study groups, he called them. Or another time, "cells." I was still at the back of the room. I had Gear Nob on one side of me, and Fats on the other, which was fine with me, even though Fats might have stood a bath a little more often, and copied off me most of the time. Anyways, Mr. Legget didn't get much taught the rest of the day, what with everybody talking and trying to figure out why he did what he did. Or else trying to figure out why they weren't sitting with the people they put down on their list. And that's pretty well the way it went into December, with us in teams of three for the rubber fights and armpit-farting contests, and Mr. Legget not getting much taught.

It wasn't till January that things changed, Mr. Legget changed. It was just before that, I guess, that the worst thing happened to him that had happened so far, just the last day before Christmas — Billy Waters standing up to him, standing over him it was, with all his arms and legs sticking out of his clothes, him having grown four inches in the last year or so. He was just in one of his bad moods and had been making so much trouble all day even Mr. Legget couldn't ignore it. He told Mr. Legget where he could go when he tried to send him down to the office. He said Mr. Legget could try and make him go if he wanted. And you could see after Billy said it he was planning to stay where he was — he was just waiting for somebody to *try* and move him, anybody could tell that. But Mr. Legget didn't do anything. He just let Billy stand there, let him swear some more when he could see Mr. Legget wasn't going to do anything. And even let the other guys in Billy's study group swear some too. Then he went back to teaching. It slowed him up for a while, you could see he wasn't teaching as fast as usual. And you could see his hands shaking a bit when he tried to write something on the board a half-hour later. But still, I thought it was a pretty good move, letting Billy stand there. I was even thinking that maybe it wouldn't be so bad staying after school some time after all, if he asked me some time and I wasn't going hunting.

It was different though when he got back in January from Christmas vacation. First day back, you could tell something was different. I thought it was just from everybody being away and then getting back together again, but no that wasn't it. It was like he'd just been waiting for a good long time to come around so he could think.

It didn't take long for somebody to start acting up. It was Billy Waters again, him still feeling pretty big from having gotten away with swearing at a teacher only a couple of weeks before. It was just a piece of rubber he threw at Fats because Fats was burping at him up at the pencil sharpener. But Mr. Legget saw it, and he came right for him. I forgot to say he was sitting *behind* his desk then, in a chair. Maybe that's what I thought was different. He was anyways, and nobody even saw him open the drawer in it, but he must

THE SAD EYE

have, because when he got to Billy he had a strap in his hand. And Billy got it there, right in the classroom, not even out in the hall like other teachers would do it. And that was that. He went crazy strapping people after that. Somebody else got it that day, I forget who, and at least one person pretty well every day after. But that wasn't even the thing about it — there were lots of teachers that gave out the strap a lot. I guess what it was was that he started to really like giving it out. He never gave it to anybody right in class again after that day, but I got it a couple of times out in the hall, and all the rest of the guys, sometimes two or three of us waiting our turn. You could see how much he liked it, you could tell from his face — that's where you looked when you got it, not at your hands, if you wanted to keep a stiff upper lip like they say. Not that you even had to do that to tell. He'd wind up like a baseball pitcher, his arm swinging around two or three times, and I'm not lying, when the strap would hit your hand his feet would jump up an inch or so off the floor. We all decided later he was the hardest strapper in the school, even if he was pretty little. We all pretty well hated him after that.

But that's not what I meant to tell about, Mr. Legget and the strap. There's not much more to it anyways — the class was pretty quiet until in April when he quit and got the job at the grocery store. That was just before the day we all spent being shown around the high school and then filling out the form telling what program we were going into. And after that, when Mr. Ruttle took over, it was pretty much the same. I guess the only exciting thing that happened was that thing with Scotty Boyd, just before Mr. Legget left. And that wasn't exciting, it was just kind of strange.

It was that committee thing — that's what he called it after he stopped the six of us after school one day. He said: "This is a committee." He was sitting up there on the edge of his desk like he was one of those chairmen or something, or a judge, only he had on his purple jacket. He made us pull six desks up around in half a circle in front of him. Then he told us again: It was a committee. It was about Scotty Boyd. About him getting beat up all the time. About him coming home after school every day and his mother finding bruises all over him. He said it all slow like that, like we were too stupid to understand.

All this wasn't much news to us, about Scotty Boyd. Blubber Bird was what we called him. It was his own fault, everything that happened to him.

The thing was, Blubber Bird was such a dummy. He was about six-foot tall and must have weighed about two hundred pounds — most of it stomach. One of the things about him was that he missed school a lot. Not that he skipped out, or had to work on a farm or anything — he lived in town. We decided that all he'd do was just tell his mom he didn't feel like going — not with all of us ruffians around — and she'd let him stay home. He never went out hunting or anything, and in the summer he'd never go out skinny-dipping in the Brickyard Pond. And it wasn't as if he was some sickly little guy. Personally I thought if he ever stood his ground he wouldn't do so bad. I mean you'd have to get some muscles just from carrying all that fat.

Anyways, Blubber had to walk home from school every day in the same direction that most of the rest of us did. That is, when he wasn't staying behind to get extra help from Mr. Legget to catch up for all the days he missed. It was only natural that he was going to get pushed around a bit in the snow the same way everybody else did. It's just that he was more clumsy and not so good at pushing back. So he got pushed down more often. I guess it got to be a kind of tradition even that old Blubber had to get his face washed in the snow and his notebooks scattered around in the slush. But it wasn't as if we held him every night and worked him over with brass knuckles or something. He just must have bruised easy.

Probably it was him staying all the time after school that got him into the worst trouble, hiding out so he wouldn't get pushed down. It just made it worse for him the rest of the time.

That was Blubber anyways, and that's what this committee thing was about — him getting beat up, which wasn't even true. Then Mr. Legget was saying a lot of stuff about what the committee was for and everything, but I didn't really hear it. For a long time I just sat there, spreading out in my desk, sticking out my legs as far as I could, and pretending to look out the window. It was a pretty bright day and I knew that the rest of the guys, the real guys, were out somewhere, maybe outside the school, or maybe gone on to Hutch's Pond hunting without me.

The thing was, I shouldn't have even been there, right from the start. There weren't any of the other guys there, not really. There was Larry Lachance, the guy I'd almost got in a fight with back at the beginning of the year. There was Jack Kellog and Jim Weatherby, who were alright, but lived on farms and didn't get into town much. There was Billy Kingston too. He was part of the gang, but kind of weak and afraid and we all used to tease him a lot. And there was Gloria Simpson. I don't know what she was doing there, except she was always a pretty good kid, and she'd never take too much crap from the guys. She was sitting right across from me in the little half circle and with my legs stretched out I was almost touching her feet. What I'm trying to say is I wasn't really like the other ones there. All of them, they were okay, but they weren't *really* okay. It wasn't like I was one of those guys that just sit quiet all day long. I'd stood up and made noise and told jokes in class sometimes, and held my own with the rest. I'd been down for the strap like the rest of the other ones, the ones who weren't there. More than some. For sure more than the ones he'd asked to stay behind. And the thing was, I was pretty sure I knew why he'd asked me to stay in the first place. It was all because of the lunch hours.

I was one of the few guys, I mean the *real* guys, in the class who stayed at school for lunch. I had to, my house being way on the other side of town, just inside the town limits. And the thing was, it would get pretty boring, what with just some girls and a few dummies from my class there in the lunch room, and a bunch of little kids starting from grade five and up yelling and screaming around. And Jack Kellog and Jim Weatherby, who kept to themselves and never said much. So pretty much from September I'd been slipping down to the library room on my lunch hours and getting some book to pass the time until the other guys got back from having lunch at home. Well really, I guess now that I think about it, I'd been doing it for as long as I can remember, way back in the younger grades. It's just that nobody ever gave me a hard time about it before. It was only Mr. Legget that ever did.

It was once back in December when it was his turn to have the lunch room. I wasn't doing anything really. I just had the book down on my lap like I always did so that nobody would know what I was doing unless they took a really hard look. It was hard enough to read anyways, what with him walking back and forth at the front of the room, humming hard but then sometimes stopping, so that you never knew where he was. I was finally getting to a good part when I looked up and there he was, so close that I could see where one of the buttons was undone on his shirt and the yellow chalk underneath his fingernails and ground into his fingerprints. He started up all about it, of course, making a fuss and talking loud, asking about what I was reading and all, all the other kids turning around to watch, thinking I was in trouble and there might be some excitement. And to make it worse, it was a kids' book that I had really, with a picture of ships and whales and things on the cover, not that it was any of his business to begin with. So I told him the name — it was *Moby Dick* — you know, just to get rid of him, only he started to make a bigger fuss out of it, wanting to talk about it because it turned out he really liked the book himself, he'd read it when he was my age and read it again every two years, he said. And he'd spent some time out on fishing boats. The only reason I got it out in the first place was because I liked reading books about ships and the sea, and that was the only thing they had left that I hadn't read down in the library. I was sort of thinking about something like that for a career, you know, maybe hiring on with one of the Great Lake freighters or something when I got old enough. So he went on and on, the rest of the dummies in the room still straining their ears to hear if I was catching shit or not, and him saying names out loud that didn't sound so bad when you read them — Captain Ahab, The Great White Whale, Tashtego — but sounded like cartoon names when you said them out loud, especially when he said them. I just kept my head down through the whole thing, studying my baloney and lettuce sandwich like it was the most important thing on earth. Finally I think he got the message, because I could see out of the side of my eye that he'd finally stopped waving the book around that he'd pulled out of my hands by that time. And then he stopped talking. And he was looking at me, who he was supposed to be talking to in the first place, not giving some sermon on *Moby Dick*. He had a funny look in his face and I figured he wasn't too pleased, that he was going to give me a hard time about not listening to him, and I was going to have to stand up to him — you know, say something really smart-assed to him, what with all the dummies watching — and then have to spend the rest of the lunch hour down at the principal's office waiting to get the strap. But he didn't say anything for a while, just crossed him arms, so that you could see where the ridges of corduroy were worn down on his elbows. Finally I said to him that I had to get back to eating my lunch; and he said Ya and went up to the desk at the front of the room. I felt kind of bad about it for some reason. After that, it seemed like he always kept an eye on me, even though I never did read again when he had the lunch room.

So like I said, I figured that was the reason he had me there with the others that day. He had me pegged as some kind of junior version of him or something, and I was just trying to hide it. And the whole thing had to do with squealing on the others, I knew it from the beginning.

So there we were, the six of us, just standing around at first while the others were putting on their coats to go home, giving us the stare. And then us having to drag the chairs around in front of him at his desk, like I said. I wanted to be there about as much as I wanted to do my math homework that night, right? And after I found out what it was about, there was about as much chance of me helping him as there was of that homework getting done. I mean it kind of felt good for a minute, being picked. But then I realized who all else was there and what it was probably all about. And if there's one thing you don't do that's to squeal on another guy, that much I know. So I just sat there, trying to look bored, and fooled around trying to kick Gloria's foot with the toe of my shoe.

After he got done telling us what the meeting was for, and some other things I wasn't paying attention to, he stopped talking. He stopped talking for a long time, and there was this big quiet with everybody breathing and the red second hand on the classroom clock going around even slower than it usually did. You could see how it was. It was him against us, us and all the other guys who weren't even there. After a long time when nobody said anything, I knew that's just what we had to do — just keep our mouths shut. There wasn't anything he could do about that. So we waited and he waited. He was humming and rocking and pulling on his sleeves, looking a lot like he did before Christmas — I didn't really notice it before, but he'd stopped doing a lot of that stuff after the holidays. But it was different too, his lips were scrunched tighter together with him not saying anything, and that thing with his arms crossed up, it looked more like in the movies when somebody's getting ready for a fight. But I thought probably it was just the situation we were in, and us being real up close to him. I started wondering if maybe he was going to start going easier on the strap. I guess my mind started wondering, it being so long without anybody saying anything.

Finally though, he did say something. And it was kind of a shock because he said it so loud after all that quiet, and because he swore. "What the hell...," he said, like I said, real loud. And then he changed it. "Just what...just WHAT... Did he *ever* hurt *any* of you guys?" real slow like that, and his elbows looking like they were going to pop through his sleeves any minute.

Most of the rest of them were scared, or at least you could see they were ready to start talking to him if he asked. Gloria, right across from me, pulled her feet in underneath her and she was leaning over her desk like she was getting set for something. Jim Weatherby's mouth was opening and closing like he was practising to say something if he had to. I knew I had to say something — it was all getting reported back to the guys some way, I knew, and I had to do something to stick up for them. So I said a really stupid thing, you know, one of those things that you remember sometimes in bed at night and your face gets all hot just thinking about it. I said, Neither did Jack The Ripper. And then I made it worse, trying to explain — I meant like if he was still alive, or something like that. I didn't really know why I said it, and I still don't. All I know is I was sorry right away after, be-

Landlock

cause nobody laughed, and because he was giving me that same look he'd given me before when I told him I had to eat my lunch. I don't remember much about what he said after that. He was waving his arms around and there was a lot of talk, but I kind of scrunched back in my seat and didn't say another thing.

It was only a couple of weeks after that he quit. And maybe a couple more before you started hearing stories of him, a teacher, getting this job here at the IGA. Nobody could figure why he didn't go back home where he came from, or at least get a better job. For a while there was a run on chips and pop from kids stopping in to look at him and them having to buy something.

And now for some reason I don't feel much like going on in the store, just in case you know, even though Mom's going to be at the door waving soon, and making some bigger kind of fuss if I pretend I don't see her or try and act like I've gone to sleep or something down here on the seat. It's just that I don't feel much like going in, just today. Probably she won't be out for another while yet.

You know, there's just one thing I've been trying to figure out — I end up thinking about it every time sitting out here these past couple weeks. I know what happened to Scotty Boyd — he kept on getting pushed down in the snow for the rest of the winter, and in the mud in the spring, and I guess he kept on getting bruises even though we never heard anything else about it. After Mr. Legget left, we got a substitute teacher for the last little while of school — a real tough guy who'd throw you against the blackboard as soon as look at you, and who'd make you stand for hours with your forehead against a wall, and come and grind it into the wall if you moved a muscle. That was Mr. Ruttle, and he stayed on after we left for high school, so our record for having gone through two teachers, including Miss Feldon in grade seven, was pretty safe forever. Besides, there was never another grade eight class like ours, with all those tough guys in it. A lot of those guys are over at the technical school out in the country now, the one that only goes to grade ten. Or else they're hanging around here at the high school in town, skipping out half the time, and hanging around the Dairy Bar smoking cigarettes. Most of them are just waiting till they turn sixteen so they can quit and get jobs. I don't know. I guess I'll stay around for a while, I can't see myself working at the car factory in the city much. Not that it's much better in high school. I didn't much like the Shop subjects all us guys signed up for back at the end of grade eight. I'm not too great in math and there's a lot of that in Shop. The problem is there's a lot of it in Sciences too, and even in Biology, and that's what I was thinking I might be — a marine biologist. Like I say, mainly I want to try and get my licence this summer and maybe get a car. Do some travelling or something. After that I don't really know what I want to do.

Oh, that thing I've been trying to figure out. Like I said, I know what happened to Scotty. And it didn't hurt him any that I can see — he's in the same high school I am right now, in the technical program, four years. Probably be making eight or nine dollars an hour in a machine shop by the time he's out. The thing I was wondering, just trying to remember, is if we ever did get around to *deciding* to do something to stop Scotty getting beat up back in grade eight. It just kind of bugs me, not being able to remember exactly. I'm not even positive what Mr. Legget expected us to do if we did decide.

It's not important anyways. I got lots of other stuff on my mind.

*F*our-Poster

It's a fight, that's for sure.

Aerobics class Mondays, Wednesdays and Thursdays. Dumbbells almost every night, but only one set, it should be three. The Nautilus again is what I should really do. I've still got muscles from last time. I popped them in the mirror for Edward, bra on to cover the stretch marks and gym shorts, that cream doesn't work at all, expensive too. Edward just laughed and did a set of Tai Chi to show me how. He teased me again about wearing makeup even to work out, I don't know how it first came up in the conversation. It's true it doesn't fit in with the lifestyle, but I just told him — I've got basically not great skin, what can I say? He just laughed some more.

Just when things start to go right something bad happens. But it's not too bad.

Something's been wrong with Slip. He wouldn't tell me what at first, but I could tell something was wrong when he picked up the kids. He knew I'd been seeing someone and I thought that had to be it, but he said no but he couldn't talk about it. This is standing up to my knees in snow talking through the car window because he won't come in, probably can't stand to be that close to me. Naturally the kids pick up this stuff. It's not fair. I start seeing a nice guy, get my life together, and Slip is falling apart. Slipsliding away, like the song. Finally I see him at the video store and he talks there of all places. He's depressed he says. He's been thinking of killing himself. He wants to talk. He's bought a gun. He threatens to stop the support money. He wants me to go to the counsellor with him.

Slip wants to get back together. Eighteen months I wait to hear that and when I do it's too late. I tell him I'll go to the counsellor to get him started, Julie thinks I'm crazy. I tell her I'm filing for the divorce, tell Edward too. I've told him a lot of the bad stuff about Slip, maybe I shouldn't. But he's a good man, doesn't say anything, says be careful, twelve years you can't turn it off like a tap, you'll hurt yourself. Says you don't *have* to burn Atlanta to free the slaves, Scarlett. Edward talks like that, especially in bed. The four-poster in the sky he calls it. Slip and I never talked in bed, especially during sex. Edward does. I like it.

This was before the doctor phoned looking for Slip. He still had this number for him, so naturally I asked. He said don't worry about him, don't come, get on with my own life and whatever Slip is going to do he'll do, it's not my responsibility. Which made me feel better and seemed funny to me and to Julie too that the doctor seemed more interested in what was good for me than Slip. They're supposed to be impartial.

Not all of this I told Edward. It's not fair he has to hear it all when we only started seeing each other. Bad enough two kids, though he's good about them, it's hard to believe. Having kids, being a mother is part of who you are, he says, you'd be someone else without them. And I like *you*. I think he's mostly saying that to make me feel better, but I think he means it too. I told him I wasn't husband-shopping.

Anyway, only so much you want to dump on a guy you like a lot but don't know real well yet.

Although Slip and I were married twelve years and how well did I know him for it to come like a bomb when he walked?

It's funny how you can not think about things when you have to. Deep down I must have known this thing with Slip was coming, I must've. After he left I was going out every night, aerobics, lectures, meetings, movies, supper, a fortune in babysitters, and it was mainly to keep the depression away. Which is another way of saying not thinking certain thoughts. And like now, that business with the gun. It's been bothering me and I've been wanting to think about it but even wanting to I've kept it pushed back, like one of those margerine containers in the bottom of the fridge I keep meaning to look at. Edward teases me about those too. He took a carrot and kept poking them one night like he was afraid they were going to explode or

Slip has bought a gun.

I told Edward. To kill *himself*, I said.

I know, Edward says, I never thought anything else. Meaning he never thought Slip planned to break in one night while we were making love and murder us. Meaning it never crossed his mind, any more than it did mine. Which is me being nasty because it did cross my mind. I know Slip enough I can say for sure he'd never do it. But it crossed my mind anyway and that's the same way it must've crossed Edward's because he knows Slip only through me and probably has an even worse version than the real one. Our good sense says it would never happen, but you think it anyway but that thinking doesn't count. So we can both say it never crossed our minds.

Julie says the only reason Slip said all that stuff was because I caught him looking at the X-rated movies.

I'm rambling on.

Last weekend was our two-month anniversary. The first time Edward and I slept together I was on my period. It was funny, we'd been out a couple of times but never even kissed. Then we did and it felt good but also strange since there was nothing to stop us going as far as we wanted. Not like dating in high school. The first kiss was like going over a cliff, there was nothing between us and bottom. Well maybe there was, maybe I even planned it that way a bit. When things get hot and Edward says maybe we should go up to the bedroom, I have to say — two problems. First I don't have anything and second I'm on my period anyway. He didn't have anything either. It seemed too sleazy to be walking around with condoms in his pocket he says. But then he thinks and says maybe the second problem could cancel out the first. Which to be honest was what I was kind of thinking myself, except I didn't want to go into a biology lesson. I didn't tell him I'd never done it before on my period, Slip always thought it was too messy. Edward didn't mind at all. He even went down there with his tongue. I wasn't real heavy, well fairly heavy by the time he got things stirred up.

So it seemed like a celebration this time and I admitted to him about never having done it this way with anyone else. He said it was nice to be the first I'd done something with in bed. He really did seem pleased by the idea and I don't think it's really sunk in yet that he's only the second I've ever done anything with in bed. Afterwards I got up to put a Tampax in and to get some wine and something to eat. We've got into the habit of eating and drinking afterwards, just raw vegetables and cheese and things, and talking, we're always going to see the sun rise but never quite make it.

This time though, going downstairs I couldn't help but think of Slip and his gun. I had a perfectly clear picture of him sitting in the dark in the living-room chair with the gun on his knees, maybe having a glass of wine. I'd remembered to turn the lights out but a CD was still playing, locked on Repeat, Muddy Waters because Edward gave it to me, build up my CD collection. Baby, I needs your love, and I could imagine Slip there in the dark mouthing the words to the unfamiliar kind of music, tapping time on the gun stock.

That was fast, Edward says when I get back with the tray. He's got a Roots sweatshirt draped around his shoulders because it's cold, I really should get the attic insulated, and he's got some of my blood smeared on his cheek like war paint. I've been walking around naked, but I put on my flannel robe for eating, it never stays on long. I get in bed and tell him about who I didn't see downstairs.

"Naked body of Nicholsby man," he says, writing the news story for his hometown paper a thousand miles away. "Found shot to death in home of Sally Siren-of-Sydlington Adams. Ms Adams, world renowned looker, also killed, was also found naked. Police spokesmen were quoted as saying, Hubba, Hubba."

Something like that. He went on a bit longer, maybe a bit too long, making fun of his accomplishments by saying them how this newspaper would. I don't know if he did it to take my mind off worrying or his own. But when he stopped the house was so quiet, the portable heater ticking and humming, the wind howling outside. The two of us seemed not big enough to fill the bed let alone the room or the house. I wanted to tell him about the blood on his cheek but I couldn't bring myself to say anything. I felt like if I wanted to get up, even to go down the hall and check the kids, the effort would be like fighting a blizzard, it would have seemed like miles, leaning into the wind and cold, blinded by snow. I had a picture of myself doing just that. Holding Edward, feeling his chest against my face and his arms around me, helped a bit.

Don't fret Scarlett.

That's when I started tickling him. He'd told me before he wasn't ticklish, but I knew it was a lie by the way he tensed up when I tried it. I'd already told him how ticklish I was, how in school the kids used to hold me down and tickle me till I cried or peed myself. He said he remembered kids doing the same thing, especially to girls, he didn't like it, it was a power thing, to make someone else lose control of their body. Edward's read a lot and is serious about some peculiar things.

"Hmpf. Hmpf Hmpf Hmpf," Edward says and I can see him starting to let go. It's a matter of finding just the right pressure on just the right spot.

"Stop."

Of course I'm hardly going to stop till I get him going a little, at least till he admits he's ticklish. I guess naturally he reaches over and starts tickling back.

"No," I tell him, letting off on tickling him and trying to grab his wrists. I really *do* tickle easy. "Don't please, I'll kick." I try kicking his shins, which isn't hard since they're already at my level. Edward's not much taller than me, like Slip, but he's also slender. That still leaves him with a weight advantage but I have broad shoulders for a woman and good upper body strength from the weights. The kicking gets him off balance a bit and with all my strength holding his wrists I can keep his hands pushed away from my ribs.

"Are we wrestling now?" He's laughing but I think the question is part serious. Once or twice before we've played around and I have an idea my arms might be as strong as his or nearly. "And in this corner," he starts but he's still laughing and having to try pretty hard and I keep kicking, keeping his hands pushed down nearly to my hips. He throws a leg over mine, pinning me, then has my legs in a scissors hold, my robe tangled up around my bum.

"Don't, stop," I tell him again. I've been holding him off pretty good but his arms are longer, he has more leverage and weight and he seems to get stronger the more he laughs like Sampson with his hair, but I guess he was stronger all along. He gets my wrists in one hand, tickling me till it feels like I'm going to pee. I'm struggling as hard as I can, laughing till

Four-Poster

I can hardly breathe, fighting as hard as I can against this man I don't really know at all except he's stronger than me I can see that, should have known even with the weights. He has me pinned, I can't move, I'm helpless and my wrists are pinched and he's making me cry. Why are men always like that?

"Stop. You're hurting me."

He stops. Finally.

"You hurt me," I tell him, rubbing my wrists. "I'm going to have bruises."

"I'm sorry. I thought you wanted to play."

"Not so rough. I hate being tickled."

"That's not true. You've been begging me to tickle you for weeks. You kept bringing it up."

"I never did. I told you. When I was little the kids used to hold me down and tickle me till I cried. I told you that."

"Sally. This is ridiculous. You started out tickling me."

"You're not ticklish. I didn't hold you down."

"You wanted to wrestle. You thought you were stronger than I was and you wanted to find out."

I didn't think he realized that part.

"I didn't want to be pinned down."

"You wanted to win."

"Next time I suppose you'll want to use ropes. Do all men like that kind of thing?"

Naturally I've gone too far. He lays on his back not saying anything. Slip used to do that.

"You're offended."

"No." The lights are out by now, the wine bottle and food tray on the floor. There's a damp spot on the sheets and my privates are scratchy with dried blood, I imagine his are too. It's quiet again and I'm afraid he's said all he's going to say.

After a minute he says, "I feel like a bully. I hurt my wife, not physically. It's one thing I never wanted to do again . . .

this is ludicrous." He sighs, a small sound against the howling of the wind, but big enough.

"Did, um, Slip hurt you?"

"Not intentionally."

He laughs, but not with humour. Then he just lays on his back not saying anything, like Slip used to, but I guess we both did, listening to the wind against the downstairs screen door, our ears straining. Neither of us admitting we're listening for thieves, rapists, men with guns. Wounded wives maybe. Listening to hear if the kids are okay. Listening to Muddy Waters singing over and over again the throaty blues. Listening for the gentle tap of a finger on the stock of a gun, which of course you never would be able to hear over the music, the wind, the tiny tinny cough of a child, or even over our own hard breathing, in and out, over and over, and never quite in rhythm. There on our backs in the four-poster in the sky. Losers, the both of us.

Among Children

Across the courtyard the sheer wall of apartment building, a few windows already yellow lit.

Below, two stories down, sparse brown grass, stiff, roots frozen in the soil between dirty patches of snow.

And in my own window my own face, blank behind a drooping moustache.

It is exceptionally cold today and it seems to be getting dark earlier than usual. Soon the two children who come to me once a week to learn "reading skills" will arrive. I hope Chris has not run ahead again to take the subway, leaving Rosaline alone to manage as best she can with the bus and the transfer to the streetcar. Rosaline has a fear of the subway, although she would not admit it; but she would also rather have somebody with her at all times.

The buzzer sounds, an ugly, abrasive noise, always a shock. I press and hold down the button on the wall to unlock the main door downstairs; but Chris continues to sound his arrival — buzz, buzz, buzzing — knowing it annoys me, though I have never given him the satisfaction of mentioning it. It surprised me at first, this pleasure he gets from causing a long-distance discomfort he can only imagine. On the positive side, I wondered if he was perhaps beyond his twelve years in his ability to abstract. And at first I spent some deal of time thinking of how he might turn this to his advantage.

Heavy tramping footsteps in the hallway now; the door

slowly opening; and there is Chris, standing, stilled for a moment — runny-nosed, cheeks cold-reddened. Hair ruffled and blond. Like his sister's. They are, were, of Dutch parentage, my tow-headed pair. So I was told.

Chris is alone and sheepishly proud of it, though he tries to cover even this. He is smileless, greetingless, and silent as is usual until he has doffed his slush-bound boots and hung up his coat — a boy wary, naturally enough, of any kind of transition. Before he can complete his transformation, the buzzer has sounded again — three short, well-spaced buzzes. As before, the ringing continues even after I press the button to release the lock on the downstairs door; but it is also different, the period of the sounds shortening, coming at longer intervals as Rosaline's short supply of confidence is sapped. She never has been quite able to make the necessary connection between the sound of the buzz downstairs and the releasing of the door latch. I send Chris downstairs in his socked feet to let her in. One more little buzz; then silence.

After a minute I hear feet in the corridor, can distinguish the light, tentative steps of Rosaline. And for a moment I have a powerful urge to embrace the embodiment of that pitiful sound; though at the same time I could almost shake her for it, and I dread her coming. This lasts only for a moment and I pass through the door to the living-room, look over lesson notes, so that Rosaline, when she enters, anxious enough already over the door incident, can remove her street clothes without my closeness to fluster her further.

They enter finally, Chris ahead, pushing the door fully open and then shutting it behind them with a light bang — confident about doors and my apartment now that he has fully shifted to his indoor personality. From my seat in the living-room I can see that Rosaline's formerly long blonde hair has been lopped to approximate one of those geometric hairstyles briefly fashionable in glossy magazines and Yonge Street malls about a year or so ago. I am glad I have a few moments to prepare a response to it. I am not very good at these minor sorts of lies.

When the children join me in the living-room I compliment Rosaline on her hair and the usual preliminary conversation begins. Chris has scored a goal in the hockey game yesterday, and his team is in first place; he is learning to play basketball. As usual Chris does most of the talking. He has become very active — healthily active — in sports during the last year and a half, according to reports. This is as opposed to the self-destructiveness (again not my term, but the social worker's) thought to underlie the numerous cuts, sprains and broken bones he used to suffer on a suspiciously regular basis. More recently, judging by remarks the pair have let slip, he seems to have become something of a bully. He is certainly cruel enough in his teasing of Rosaline when they are here; although I have been told, and I believe, that he is very protective of her at school. Nothing really changes.

Eventually I manage to work the conversation around to Rosaline. She must think hard to find something to say. Nothing has really happened to her during the week, she finally announces in her soft voice. She has gone to school, talked with her friends. And, oh yes, the creative dance class she had planned to attend with her friend has started. But she cannot go after all, on account of the cost . . . even though Chris can go away to hockey school in the summer. Immediately she is regretful now the complaint has slipped out. But even though it has, it sounds empty, without resentment. She does not blame Chris; she does not blame. I can see that they are ruining Rosaline, these foster parents. And I can see that they, or somebody, already have done so to Chris.

Amazing, my new objectivity.

It is time, finally, to get down to work. Chris, surprisingly, is the one who needs the most help, though I have only recently discovered this. He has been reading chapters from a *Hardy Boys* book unearthed from the still-boxed piles of my own books, a remnant of my own childhood. Before he reads I show him flashcards of the difficult words from the chapter, putting aside the ones he has difficulty with for him to try again afterwards. It is a method I use with both of them, although I have learned to do Chris first; he is easily bored and often will rise from whatever exercise I have set him, roaming about the sparsely furnished room, fiddling with relentless but unperceiving hands the few objects of the apartment (the knobs of the record-player, the ancient fittings of the radiator), making as much noise as he can get away with, calling for direct attention. He really does need individual, professional tutorage. But that, of course, is out of my hands: this will probably be the last time I see either of them. After the flashcards I set him to his reading.

I start to work with Rosaline now, quickly going through her cards and setting her to read. I have been having her read *Alice in Wonderland* these past couple of months, another relic picked from the boxes, left over no doubt from college days judging by its small adult-sized type and illegible margin notes, although I don't remember ever studying it. Rosaline doesn't know what to make of Alice's frequent malapropisms; and I don't really know what to do about them either. The book is hopelessly inappropriate for this use, here; is from such a distant other place and time. Too late to change now of course. And funny too, in that sadly ironic way that anything seems funny these days. Funny because, at one point, I had attempted to get a different book for her; and because it was this incident, if one must be chosen, that finally made me decide to move on, leave the city, even before the end of their school year or the beginning of mine. That afternoon shortly after Christmas; the circuitous walk through unfamiliar city streets; the library finally found, massive and new, swollen with its books. But intended exclusively for research, not for lending. I would even have considered stealing had not a sign warned of such crimes, of electronic monitoring, of certain prosecution; had I not, during my life, been conditioned to a ready belief in such signs. So I stood there in the lobby, bewildered as any child. A rubbie in a lobby chair, sated with the heat of the building, blew long warm farts; the stiffened clerk at the desk sniffed — at him, at the ragged cuffs of my jeans and parka, or from an oncoming cold. The twin turnstiles guarding the stacks remained locked in position. And I decided it was time, once more, to leave. I gave the Super notice that very afternoon.

Before long Chris is finished, having rushed through, skimming the pages. He will not remember what he has read; most of the words with which he was unfamiliar will remain so. I go through the cards again, and it is as I supposed. We do a grammar exercise together and although Chris is still restless, I am the one who grows bored. I do not wish, have never wished really, to teach him the mechanics of the English language. It is another language I would have taught, one of trust, of forgiveness, of risk, of I don't know what — one, I finally realize, I do not know myself. I finish with him and set him to do a phonics lesson.

By now Rosaline has finished her chapter of *Alice*. She looks bewildered but does better than Chris with her flashcards. I think she knows even more of the words than is apparent, because, when she is unsure, she refuses even to try to answer, to actively take part in her own humiliation. Not an unwise practice, this slight self-defense, I suppose, given her life, given the necessity of living with Chris. By this point I no longer force her.

Nearly finished with Rosaline now, I notice Chris squirming and restless in the position he has taken on the floor, and I am fascinated by the way his discomfort is transmitted to and assimilated by Rosaline, her delicate lips, the sensitive blue-veined flesh of her mouth, twitching like antennae. For a dangerous moment I feel urged to do something for her, to entertain — but the moment quickly passes. I have already given over such possibilities. For even though they were impressed at first by me, the sparse, largish apartment, by the numerous oversized books overflowing their boxes, even though this unexpected event had filled us all with such enthusiasm those first few weeks, it had soon worn off, as all such things do. And although I can imagine even now how they might scream with delight and love me if they only knew what fine and funny caricatures I could draw of them, of myself, types of their teachers and fat old women in the street; even though I can imagine this, I would not do it. Neither, of course, would I show them my work — the water-colour of Chris at his most sullen, the numerous studies of Rosaline — or even the bare paraphernalia of my craft ... trade rather. They would find it ... interesting, at first. But inevitably, finally, they would become bored as they must with gimmicks and fraud. No, I will not entertain. I threaten Chris back to work and finish with Rosaline.

It is nearly time for them to leave now and I shorten the time I usually allot for our last activity of the session. The three of us are to write short descriptions of some person or thing within a set time limit. I signal to begin; but five minutes pass and our pencils are still poised over the papers, less than a handful of words drawn among us. A brief laugh of relief unites us for a moment when we realize our common dullness and we decide to end it for the evening.

At the door the children dress quietly and deliberately for the cold trip home. I bid them good-bye, firmly close the door behind them, and travel the two strides into my small kitchen — my kitchenette, I think they call it — which faces the doorway. Chris's departing buzz from downstairs startles me slightly, but does not bother me.

I extract a bottle from the cupboard; am annoyed only passingly by the grease from the cupboard door which rubs off on my knuckles and which I in turn rub off with a dank washcloth. Cold cubes from the refrigerator clatter momentarily in the bottom of a glass, their sharp edges becoming rounded by the first contact with the warm liquor. I bring both bottle and glass with me into the living-room and flop into the by now well-defined hollow of my colourless Salvation Army chair. Experimentally I sip the Scotch, find it a little rough, not as yet sufficiently diluted by the melting ice. But I can wait; I am so relieved that the session is over, that everything is finally over.

I realize by now, of course, that I have never really helped these kids, even with their reading problems — not that I ever believed I could, in that area, my original volunteering to help kids with Art being translated by the powers-that-be into a willingness just to help, reading being where it was most needed. But it wouldn't have mattered: I am no teacher, no artist; am tradesman at best. The correspondence course I "teach" is proof of that: my fine and objective criticism of the assignments (watch proportions; practise the grid method; try for less equine noses); the fairest marking — all conducted by mail. And the contract to teach summer school at the technical college in London is further proof, job training of the greatest number for the most money in the shortest time. Job training, I must now admit, that was always there in the background, my acceptance of the work implied long before the offer was official, at no time really considered revocable — my bread and butter, don't ya know — my ever-present escape hatch. God knows what I was trying to do, taking on these kids half-way through a long winter meant to be given over to making it or breaking it, whatever that means. God knows; some part of me must have too.

It is completely dark out now. I should draw the curtains, but it doesn't really matter. Let the interested public see what they will. I decide to have one last, slow drink. To time it I light a cigarette. On impulse I set it in the ashtray and light a second, laying it cross-wise on top of the first. I have done this before, I recall; the effect is weird, creating as it does the obstinate illusion that somebody else, some careless other who has just left the room, will return shortly. I watch the two in the ashtray for what does not seem to be a very long time, my eyes watery from smoke or concentration as finally they burn across each other. One usually burns faster than the other, the result of air movement or varying densities of tobacco. But at the end, as always, they are both short trails of ashes. I swallow the last of my drink and am ready to begin.

It is sheer habit of course, this nightly dragging out, resurrection of my "works" from beneath the stack of newspapers under my chair; the laying out of them in front of me on the floor, examination of the days' fruits, arranging and rearranging of them in stacks like some on-going game of solitaire. And, although this too is part of the ritual, I am freshly surprised by how little I have produced, as though there ought to be some automatic, magical return upon the months' investment.

I shuffle first through the thickest stack containing, with one exception, the numerous pencil sketches, studies of Rosaline. Reluctantly but directly I select the single exception, the folder containing the first preliminary water-colour of her, a confrontation I have been putting off since the few days ago when it was finished. As I suspected, she has died as she dried, as the paint set. She is a powdery grinning Degas dancer with none of the haughty naivete to her, the flesh more closely akin to the upholstered stuffing of my shabby chair than to anything living. Deliberately I leave the folder open in front of me: evidence.

The next I lay hands upon is a sketch of Chris, which is not too bad really, though tediously realistic — the features set, expression closed and neutral, except for the lines of the mouth hinting at once as they do of both cruelty and fear. By chance the drawing has escaped from the separate pile of his other studies into the stack of sketches of my "ideal" man, men, all earlier works begun at first for simple lack of models, and continued, more than for any other reason, as aid and abetment to a long period of self-pity. The idea was a joke. Of sorts. Not that anyone would recognize the original notion on which the irony depends, though some of the lines and shading, the musculature, are a fair rendering of the classical Greek model. But as for the rest: the stone blind eyes are so wide they could belong to a comic-strip character. Nobody would comprehend the mutilated hands, the clenched jaw, the slightly distended forehead, bulging as though crammed; nor would anyone recognize the snow and ice in which the legs are mired for what they are: snow and ice. I am indeed a caricaturist.

But the telephone next to me on the floor is ringing. I drop Chris's sketch, which I find I am still holding in one hand, on the floor to attend. Mr. Johnston, someone says as I raise the receiver; I agree with him: yes. We have a problem with James. I, cautiously formal, say that I think perhaps there is some confusion, that although he has my name right, I know no James. And when, still confused, he asks, I explain to him that no, this is not the Children's Aid, that although I do, I have, worked with them, I am only a volunteer. When finally this is clear, he continues to talk, exorcising his grievances through the simple making of sound.

It turns out shortly that this is the final straw for him, that this James has been causing numerous problems — fighting the other children and even him — that now he has run away from the group home. And, once it is realized that I have only to do with Rosaline and Chris, other things turn out as well. It turns out, for instance, that Chris and Rosaline have other names, unfamiliar names so casually conjoined with their first ones by this stranger. And it turns out it is only Chris who is of Dutch parents, that I must have misread some report or other, and that any similarity of looks is purely coincidental — that they are not really related, but have simply taken on the family name of their foster parents, one of whom is this man.

While I attempt to assimilate these new turnings-out we continue to chat. James, it seems, is not a permanent member of the group home the way Rosaline and Chris are. Among his many other problems, James also needs special aid learning to read (an emphasis on this since it is my "subject" and hence of great interest to me). Yes, he too needs special help. And, really, isn't it a shame that a child — although at fifteen he is hardly a child, is as strong as an adult, as hard to handle — isn't it a shame that a child of that age has trouble reading street signs. It will be so hard for him in Life.

Finally, very politely, I agree with all this, thinking what an ass I have been, how of course Rosaline is not a Dutch name, and what a further ass I am to be so bothered by it. Noticing the crumpled piece of paper under one corner of the telephone, the series of numbers scratched beside the letters CA, I interrupt abruptly, relay this to him, saying, perhaps it will help, and, good-bye.

For a few minutes after I hang up, I think nothing, the active part of my mind totally disengaged. Then, as though my mind has suddenly meshed with some powerful spinning gear, I do begin to think, the notions coming fast, becoming circular: I think of childhood, my own, how very much more fortunate I was to have finally had my own parents, *private* parents; how kind they had been, how generous, to have accepted a six-year-old child, sandy-haired, but definitely over-quiet and clearly underweight, probably dirty, into their relative affluence. How they continued the kindness, the acceptance, though almost from the first he had betrayed them, the sandy hair changing insidiously to ever darker shades; how, when he became even more withdrawn, and even when he went through that hostile and rebellious stage which most children do, they continued to accept and to support, and yes, to love, even. Always so generous and supportive — so much so that even now I could live quite lavishly if I was up to a few minor banking transactions. Always so kind — so damned kind — to their only son, their single child.

But finally these thoughts cannot continue. They are surface, habitually used shelters which have worn increasingly thin now, become inadequate. Soon I slow, realize other thoughts which have been welling, waiting, only infrequently and partially acknowledged.

I think of another time, scarcely within memory, before all this, before these parents.

I can remember now the buildings and the countryside, can remember them almost better than any of the people.

I remember the farmhouse. How I would approach it from the rear towards the end of the day, passing through the desolate farmyard with its awful populous of dirty grey outbuildings.

And, almost but not quite, I can summon up the lovely black and fertile soil of the tilled fields in the spring; the weeds, tall and green and moist, in the ditches at that same time of year; how those weeds would turn golden brown with the heat of the summer, become warm and soft with the sun and with dust from the dirt road.

Almost, I can recall this. Or rather the textures of it, the feeling.

Almost. For of course not all my life then was lived among the weeds, in the soil, despite the fact that most days I would leave the house early in the morning and, regardless of hunger, would not return until dark — passing as far as I could from the grey wooden outbuildings of which I had formed such a terror, towards the lighted windows in the rear of the farmhouse and the goal of the creaking, paintless back door. I was foolish then, being only six at the time. I was more afraid of the dark and cold of the wooden buildings than of anything that was contained in the house —

more afraid of that particular toolshed which had held me locked for most of a night, howling until I choked from lack of breath, chilling my young butt on its earth floor so that I couldn't go for a week after, even if I had dared the confines of the seldom-used privy out behind the kitchen, or the bathroom inside with its massive door — more afraid of this, than of any people.

And, too, at six I did very much love my sister, in my own selfish six-year-old way.

So I would move on past those smaller buildings towards the house which was, by that time of day, set off against the horizon, the setting sun always, it seems now, impaled at various angles on the crumbling chimney. With a sudden sense of moment which just as suddenly would pass, I would step across that line on the ground where the shadow of the house began; and then I'd rush to the back windows of the house. Standing on my toes on a rotting bale of straw at one of those windows, I'd peep through into the kitchen to make sure that only one person was there. Then, going to the door, I'd carefully but impatiently manipulate the smashed and rusting latch so that it wouldn't squeak, and, mastering that, would ease my body like a cat through the partially open door.

For a minute my sister would be unaware of me. Or at least she would pretend to be, as she peeled potatoes selected from the endless bushel in the pantry, or washed grease from the dishes which had accumulated through the day, while the supper cooked on the even greasier gas stove. At times, even now, she would then turn as she almost always had before, and pretending just to notice me, would stamp her feet up and down, moving towards me as if to chase; and I would make a show of turning to run. She would catch me, of course, her strong hands sliding up my sides and under my arms. And then she would try to lift me in the air to her, not always managing it and kneeling to hug me instead, so that my nose and eyes would be pushed against the base of her thick auburn pigtails, which later, for no good reason, I came to think of as dirtied, off-colour carrots. More and more it seemed, as that summer progressed, she had to kneel in front of me, and my face was pushed into her hair. For, although I was skinny, I suppose I must also have been growing heavier. And because, even though my need of her was so great, she herself was only ten years old.

By the time that we had hugged, the others would have become aware of us in the kitchen. Or so we thought; and in thinking so would become aware of them, which was enough to spoil it. We were too afraid. Helen would go back to her cooking, her dishes, and I, excused because of my age, would move off upstairs, travelling throughout the rooms of the second floor, slinking and quiet, and always, with a part of myself, alert.

It was out of that alertness and that silence, I suppose, that I became alert to other things. Touching, I was always touching.

That is how I came to know almost every object on the second floor, the contents of every cupboard and every drawer. I knew of the one particular cupboard filled with old china cups, knew their various patterns, the ancient tea stains inside. I knew of the broken umbrella behind the cabinet, the silky black fabric of it, and the individual threads in its weave that you could see if you looked hard enough; and I knew the single wooden sprocket, long lost from some Tinker Toy set out of somebody else's childhood, nested as it was in cobwebs beneath the chest in the big hall closet that was used for storage. Even the Bible I came to know in this way, though I did not realize that was what it was at the time. It was a big book, with a thick binding and stiff pages of illustrations between the translucent ones of type. I would run my fingers over those delicate pages of type, trying to feel the words; and so too with the illustrations. I felt if only my touch was gentle enough I could extract the figures from the bright illustrations by tracing them with my finger tips. Soon, from numerous attempts, there grew to be a greasy outline around many of the figures.

Always, too, in my investigations I would be certain to replace everything where I'd found it — the wooden toy piece in its nest, the Bible on the top of the cabinet. No one knew what I did with my time upstairs. At least, that is how it seems to me now.

It would be, then, some time well into my daily second-floor excursion before I was called for supper, a thing I dared not refuse and which at first I probably did not want to. I would descend the stairway, threading my way around the solid farmhouse furniture, and continue threading my way even in the open spaces, using up seconds, because, by then, as I neared the dining room, I would be becoming less and less hungry. When I did reach the table I would take my place next to my sister, where I would wait with my head down to my plate for her to fill it with food.

Mostly, throughout the meal, I would keep my head bowed in this way. Occasionally though, for some reason or other, I would have to look up for a moment. During these infrequent moments my eyes would quickly take in the table full of strangers surrounding me. For a time I would glimpse them in their common but disharmonious activity of eating, filling their mouths with the meal my sister had prepared. I would see The Man in his grimy, green work clothes, his hair grey-black and dirty with sweat and grease. He was seldom around except at mealtimes, because, I think, he worked someplace else during the day away from the farm. During the evenings he mostly slept, although despite that or even because of it, the skin beneath his eyes was always puffy and purplish; and the rest of his face, to me, always seemed to be like the floury stew we had to eat several times a week, that colour and texture.

Among Children

Beside The Man would sit The Lady, divided from him by the right angle of the table corner. A large dowdy woman in bright stretchy shorts, a devotee of daytime television, she would sometimes clean small portions of the living-room during the commercial breaks throughout the day, conserving her energy, it now seems, for her major effort at the end of the day of looking tired and overworked and oppressed when The Man came in. I think she was the wife of The Man and the mother of some of the numerous but often different older children around the table.

Of those other children who always seemed to be coming and going, different but perfectly interchangeable, there was one who was not these things; and it was he who my seldom uplifted eyes would catch on. Terrified but fascinated for a moment, I would watch him gobbling quartered potatoes, huge segments of carrots; look on as he crammed whatever meat there was into his mouth. And, terribly aware of my sister next to me at such moments, needing her perhaps most then, I would be unable to turn to her. I would be afraid that I might find her in the act of eating; afraid that, seeing her, I would gag on my own food, as I had before. It was not long after one of these meals with their furtive observings that I became unable at all to eat the carrots when they were put in front of me. It was not long either before my inability became generalized to all vegetables, so that my sister, when over the course of a couple of meals she noticed it, ceased to serve them to me at all, or, when that was commented on, began to transfer them to her own plate when nobody was looking.

For although I still returned to the house after my daily foragings in the countryside, although I was still afraid of the numerous grey and shadowy outbuildings, I had at least made some of the connections. Watching the oily face of that giant who sat across the table from me, that fourteen-year-old, strong from chores and school-yard fighting, aware of each shining pimple on the huge face, and aware, even if only for moments in long intervals of time, of the hand bringing to those greasy lips shovelfuls of the food which my sister had prepared — watching this, I couldn't really help but know that it was by that same hand that I had been locked in the shed for that long and cold and desperate night. And that it could happen again.

It was this last thing, more than anything else, which made me wish that he were gone — or dead, which amounts to the same idea at six years of age; this same thing, I suppose, which made me become a kind of colluder with him against my sister. Somehow I felt that she should be able to do something about the situation; and because she didn't, it made me begin to hate her. It was not an unfounded belief either, because, I realize now, the boy, with his sneaking, oily glances, must have felt too the power she had; and also hated her for it.

But although it was for what they *could* do that I hated them, I still remembered what *had* been done.

I remembered that it had been after supper one night. This was in the days when I would come in from my outings early, at five o'clock or so, because it was then that my sister would be home from school, dropped off by the big orange school bus; and it was in these days that, when she would pretend to chase and I to run, she was almost always able to lift me. We were both in her room that night, a room she shared with others I don't remember and who were not there. She was at the old school desk doing homework, while I lay on her bed, head over the edge, studying the dust beneath or involved in some other game, content to be near her. It was then when he came in, pausing for a moment, not looking at her, at either of us, walking straight to the window, and looking out as if he'd come for that very purpose. I could have told him there was nothing to be seen from that farmhouse window, I'd checked, just the darkened countryside which I knew quite well already. But somehow I knew better than to speak. It was a while before he turned to me and told me, a whitehead at the corner of his mouth threatening to burst, to get out. Which I immediately did. Because we had not been there so very long then and we were like guests — yes, guests, I remember my sister saying it. And too, of course, his size, colossal there, so close yet so unknown.

So I did go, exploring the other rooms on the upper floor which then were not so familiar. It was that night, if I remember properly, that I found the wooden sprocket in its dusty nest beneath the cabinet.

But I tired of this soon. Then, I still felt that I had some rights with my sister, especially since it was a school day and my time with her was so brief. It was nine o'clock then by the big grandfather clock in the hallway — I clearly remember the clock face, even though I may not have known what it meant at the time. It was then, anyway, that I returned to stand outside my sister's door. Then that I softly pushed the edge of the door open a finger's width, then two, wishing only to see her, and thus determine whether it would be best to surprise her or just quietly to take up my place again on the bed near her. I was not surprised by what I saw, nor was I shocked; although I was, perhaps, a little jealous. But mostly I was just curious as I watched the two of them at the school desk, he with his buttocks leaned against it, facing slightly away from me towards the window, and my sister kneeling before him. It was only after I noticed the way he held the back of her head, one of the red pigtails wrapped around his hand, forcing her to him; only after I realized her muffled chocking sound, that I began to be a little afraid. And it was only a single moment, when all at once the boy's shoulder and arm, his whole body, went rigid and then were shaking with spasm; when my sister, her mouth crammed with him, began choking, eyes wide with breathlessness; and only when those eyes caught sight of me at the door, that it finally came to me that something important was happening, something which required some sort of action, however much I had no idea what that action was.

It seems now that all this occurred in a single moment. It seems that it took even less time than that for the giant of a boy to recover himself, for him to sweep the room with a gaze as though somebody might be there inside, and finally for that gaze to rest on me at the doorway. So fast was it, for all its flashing vividness, I barely remember the lightning fingers fastening the buttons and buckles of his trousers, my sister coughing and perhaps quietly sobbing on her bed with her knees drawn up to her, and his demands of whether I had seen anything, whether I would say anything. And it was confusion, simple confusion from a lack of time to think, which made me steadfastly nod and keep nodding my head in agreement with everything he said, not realizing the equally easy required and saving gesture. It was this confusion, I suppose, as well as my nature, which kept me silent as he half lifted, half dragged me down the stairway and past the backs of The Man and The Lady in the living-room, the one almost certainly asleep in front of the murmuring television, and the other lulled to an equal oblivion by her watching; confusion mixed with a kind of blind optimism learned no doubt from my sister which made me entertain, however fleetingly, the idea that it was all some kind of not-very-fun game which might even get better, at the very time he was slamming shut the door to the toolshed so that it might teach me, so that I might finally learn my lesson. The moment was complete by the time I did gather my wits, before I did realize and try to get out, and before the long night actually began.

The days seemed countless after this point — perhaps a month or so of them — days filled with such excursions into the countryside as I have mentioned, such suppers, filled with my sister's inconsistent affection and with nights when I would no longer go to her room but would continue my inspection, my confirmation, of the others. I have no idea if, within that time, the boy repeated his visit to my sister's room; and of course I do not know what happened after that. Before the summer was over, I was taken into the home of the people who gave me their name. I do not recall any precise leave-taking of my sister during that time, if indeed one took place.

I was still six then and was enrolled in a school in the city that fall, a year later than I should have been, I later found out. I did well there, receiving help with my homework from my new parents, encouragement in those areas which I seemed to like, and, later, the gifts of modelling clay, charcoals, the special lessons which enabled me at an early age to begin manufacture of the numerous winter landscape scenes which always managed to win prizes in my teens. All these things I received, things very expensive, which only a couple with means, a couple with a single child, people who had made such a conscious effort to obtain that child, could afford.

I found, too, that generally I liked my new world in the city, with so many new things to observe and explore. And, as I have said, my world seemed to favour me, as I later found it often does children who are silent, reasonably handsome, and quick-minded. I realized something of this even then I suppose, knew somehow that, for all my withdrawal, my rebelliously changing hair colour, and my probable uncleanliness, I was a far better catch than a bony ten-year-old girl with red pigtails who already resembled the over-worked scullery maid she was made to be. But at six, or seven, or even later, when one has been familiar with the dark, cold places of punishment, one does not protest any but the most personal and blatant injustices. And of course memory, while I have discovered that it is not short, is very slow.

So it is that, only now, some time after my thirtieth birthday, certain things begin to dawn; only now that the present day and those that happened some twenty-four years ago lie side by side for comparison.

But it is too easy, too difficult. My tow-headed pair are not my sister and me. There are no parallels. Events are too different.

Chris is not like I am. It is doubtful that he will ever face any forced separation from his sister who is not his sister, or that he will participate in any but the most natural and minor violations of her. Their foster parents, so I am told, are very fond of them, and have taken in the pair as their own, albeit unofficially. And soon they will be at an age when they can make many decisions on their own, or at least it will seem that way, and that is the same thing.

No, it is doubtful in the extreme that Chris will ever be compelled to such painful penitence, such re-enactment for whatever lunatic reasons. It is doubtful that there will ever be some terrible fixed point, moment, in his life which he will be able to point to and say, yes, this is unfair and it should be rectified. Or else, if there is, it will be too late; and he will know.

Because, finally, only a fool would ever strive to touch, to alter, that which the distances of time and reality have made unapproachable; because finally no longer do stamping feet pretend to chase while others pretend to run; and because at one time they did. Because of this, I can finally take my leave.

S*toneware*

"*We'd gone to* secretarial school together, Elsa and me," my mother said. "We'd come into the City looking for work. We were trying to find a place that'd have the two of us together.

"For some reason we got held up till evening. We were walking down this street, the air-raid sirens went off, so we headed to the nearest shelter. There were some platforms set up and we were both so tired, so we lay down together and went right to sleep. I remember I took the outside — the cement walls down there would get so clammy.

"Anyway, later we woke up, the both of us at the same time. We'd rolled so I was on top of her, our faces only a couple of inches apart. Elsa, she gives this shiver, looks me right in the face — she was always a prim, pretty little thing, Elsa, the best typist in the class — looks me right in the face and says, 'FUCK.' Just like that. Hoarse, but loud so everyone heard. I'd been drooling on her all the time we were asleep. Her collar was soaked. Her one cheek was covered in drool. And I'd got her pushed right against the cold cement, snuggling up to get warm."

I laughed and poured us some more rye, then ginger ale, while my mother, heated from talking, undid some of the buttons of her sweater. It was the first time I'd ever heard her use a swear word and the first time I'd seen her even nearly drunk. I noticed an auburn lock had come askew from the lacquered hardhat of a hairstyle she had worn forever —

surely a precedent. Then I snorted again to think of my mother side by side with her prim friend. The joke was in the contrast. My mother could never have been called prim, with her big hands and large-boned body. I remembered she had never been much of a secretary either. But she had never wanted to be these things. She seemed to be enjoying her middle years and I was glad of it. She seemed to be enjoying talking to me as an adult — I'd seen her only once before in the four years since I was twenty-two — and that too made me glad.

It would be my turn to tell a story soon. We'd already exchanged several that evening, over rye and the shifting brick-patterned oilcloth on the kitchen table. And in between other talk of family, our current lives. But the story-swapping was different from just talk, a longstanding entertainment just for the two of us, begun back when I'd first started attending school.

Sitting there, listening to her talk some more of Elsa, her friend who was eventually killed in the Blitz, I remembered my first story. I had come home from school one day, during my first weeks of kindergarten. My mother had asked about my day, as she had each school day from the beginning. Usually her asking was all it took to set me off, recounting the myriad events crowding my half day away from home. This day, however, only one event filled my mind, although I was too embarrassed to tell it. Unused to waiting for permission, I had wet my pants in class. Miss Keller, my teacher and an otherwise tolerant woman, held notoriously strict views on bladder control; I had been duly swatted and sent to dry out in the tiny cloakroom adjoining the classroom. There, with little else to distract me from my humiliation, I had conducted a thorough study of a drain set in the stone floor tiles, watched it alternately back up a small puddle around itself and suck it back down again.

Stoneware

This last was the inspiration for my first story: The school had flooded, I began, hesitantly. Water had started to rise, desks and children to float. I had rushed from my seat to the front of the room, grabbed Miss Keller who had broken both arms in the confusion, bounded to her desk top and then to the safety of the suspended light fixtures over our heads. Soon acrobatic policemen had arrived and, swinging on ropes secured to the lights, rescued the other children.

It was the most exhilarating few moments of my life then, telling that story. The initial guilty twinge accompanying the lie of the flood was completely assuaged by the attention and seeming belief in my mother's face. I'd run with it after that, forgetting totally my salty, yellowed drawers. Afterwards, my mother told me the first in the long series of small incidents from her girlhood in England before and during World War II, I forget which. Some were taken from cycling trips she made into the countryside with her friends, picnics they would have there; others from rambling walking excursions through fields, basket in hand, to collect shrapnel for scrap. Possibly it involved the POW camp near where she lived, and the two or three prisoners she used to talk to through the double-fencing, for many of the later ones included this. None was ever as complicated or as fantastical as my stories, but I always accepted them as equivalents and assumed my mother meant them to be. It became a pastime with us, off and on until I was a teenager, the swapping of my present-day fantasies of heroism for verbal snapshots of my mother's early girlhood. Always it was a wholly different thing from the newsy talk we shared with the rest of the family, my father and sister Marilyn, at the supper table.

The stories, however, stopped soon after I started attending high school. I don't know why. Possibly my mother ran out of girlhood to share; perhaps the fantasies I would have invented at that time were not fit for motherly ears. My world became an intensely private one, in any case. I drifted more and more towards the fringes of the high school population, towards the few drug-takers in our small county high school, the frequently truant. I embarrassed my sister, who attended the same school, one year behind me. Once, two days before the elections, I declared my candidacy for student president. During the candidates' meeting, from the bare open stage, I made an intoxicated speech appealing for increased student rights; of course I lost by a landslide. At home, my father, a gentle, hardworking salesman, tried gently to sell me on a more stable lifestyle; then tried more aggressive means of persuasion. Naturally I hated him — for failing his mission as much as for trying — and lumped him and my mother together with the rest of the repressive regime intent on stifling me.

Eventually I drifted into university. I soon found the fringe here too. One night, near the beginning, I met a loosely organized group of poets and folk singers in the student pub. By my fourth year I was a core member of the group, was double-majoring in English and Communications, and had somehow wangled a teaching assistantship. I graded papers for a couple of professors teaching Intro Composition, and I was supposed to be available to students, almost all of them foreign, to help them with their assignments. I hadn't swapped tales with my mother in all that time.

The story I told now was of this period, my final year in university. I had decided by then that I had the stuff of great poetry within me. I'd already read maybe a dozen times at coffee houses and to small gatherings at student residences, although I hadn't published. I had finally worked up the courage, however, to submit a bundle of my work to a professor I T.A.ed for, a poet himself, whose work I admired very much. After reading it, and along with more tactful comments, he suggested that perhaps poetry and I weren't suited for each other. With that advice, he had handed me a sheaf of papers to mark, which I did, harder and probably more thoroughly than I ever had before — the mean grade was D+.

I didn't preface my tale with this information. I simply told how I found myself in my library cubicle one day, staring at the walls, the noise of hammering precluding work, the plaster dust turning my hair to grey. My wing of the library had been undergoing reconstruction for most of the school year. Despite this, I was obliged to conduct interviews there during Tuesday and Thursday mornings, if any students wished to see me.

As it turned out, the only student who regularly wanted to see me on Tuesdays — the only student who regularly saw me at all — was a plump, malodorous girl who habitually sat too close to me in my minuscule office for comfort. One of the few non-foreign students in the classes, she was a science major, some sort of mathematical wizard, attending her first year on a scholarship. She couldn't write worth a damn, however, and had received a D- on her last paper, an only slightly lower grade than those she'd been receiving all along in her one venture off the terra firma of maths and sciences.

On this Tuesday, in the middle of my explanation of why I had given her the grade, she placed a plaster-powdered hand on my leg. In a voice meant to sound enticing, she said how she would do almost *anything*, if she could only get a B. Without missing a beat I had looked at her and made the counter-proposition: if she would kindly remove her hand from my thigh and promise never to bother me again, I would give her a C. She did, I did, and I never spent another Tuesday morning in my office.

My mother thought this uproariously funny, and I poured us another. Rye — not a bad drink after the first few. I hadn't realized how much I missed it all these years, the trading of tales with my mother. I didn't know why I had decided particularly on the incident with the girl. It wasn't nearly as funny as my mother made out and was only one of dozens of similar small incidents I had unwillingly collected — the type of meaningless but stubborn memory which for no good reason would pop into mind during some otherwise pleasant, or at least neutral, idle hour. I'd had more than my share of idle hours during the several years since leaving school. I was trying to write a novel. My plan was to capture definitively the beauty and hypocrisy of the small Ontario county in which I had grown up, was how I put it to the co-worker at the prairie finance company's "house organ" where I worked as a staff writer. I would have put it at much greater length had I not discovered that he, along with the other writer there, had similar ambitions with his own home turf. If truth were known, work was stalled on the book and I increasingly spent my daily block of writing time composing and revising the jacket blurb. Now, at least, it was unlikely that the sound of that kittenish, desperate little voice in the library cubicle would ever again be among the memories disturbing my concentration.

It was late now. I absently sloshed rye up the hard insides of the bottle; it was nearly two-thirds empty. We'd covered a lot of ground in my short visit. The last time we'd seen each other had been two years ago on the occasion of my father's death. I was still somewhat estranged from the family then, hard at work on The Novel. Unable to feel anything much at the sight of my father's coffin, his face waxy and cold within, I had comforted myself with Greene's maxim that a writer must possess a sliver of ice in his heart, and I had made care-

Stoneware

ful notes. My mother, however, had grieved hard during the couple of days I was home.

Apparently my mother's grief was shortlived. She was now friends with Alvin Buchwald, a widower and former owner of the town's butcher shop. He had sold the business after his wife's death and was now building a sailboat in his basement, a longstanding dream. My mother was actually helping Alvin with some of the more delicate aspects of boat building. He could neither swim nor sail, my mother had added after telling me of Alvin's project, and she seemed to appreciate the irony as much as I. I assumed the two of them slept together; I hoped they did. There wasn't much other social life in the little town. My sister and her husband, a telephone company employee, still lived in the area. But they disapproved of her friendship with Alvin.

My mother mentioned Marilyn's disapproval shortly after I told the library story. There was no need for me to say anything in support of my mother at this point, however; and my mother didn't seem to expect it. She knew. She wasn't complaining, she said.

It was time for sleep. I'd driven two days across endless plains, another one through tortuous Shield country, over eighteen hundred road miles for this short visit with my mother. An agoraphobic impulse. Now I had the return journey to make, back to the flat and open West, to a fast frantic fresh start on The Novel, then back to the Organ again, my short vacation over. I had some new ideas I wanted to get written down that night before I lost them. Already I was anticipating my old bedroom, wondering if it had shrunk any smaller since my visit two years before.

My mother poured us each another drink, slopping the ginger ale and accidentally shifting the puddled oilcloth even further on the table so that it made a tent over my knees. Oh, well, when again, I thought. But I told her this would have to be the last drink.

"I just wanted to tell you," she said. Then she changed it. "Did I ever tell you? About how your father and I got married?"

Like most children I had asked and been told the story of how my parents first met. Theirs was in fact a rather more romantic story than most and I intended to incorporate it in The Novel.

My father had enlisted in the Navy near the end of the war, and while waiting for the call to action which never came, he and his guitar, his oldest companion, found a large and ready audience. When he came home, he joined a band which played in local hotels and at dances. Every friendly gathering at our house during my childhood had been conducted to the tune of the old favourites: "Blue Spanish Eyes," "Has Anybody Seen My Gal?" that sort of thing. As for my mother, after the war she and her family emigrated to Canada. She soon found work as a secretary and one night visited a dance hall with a girlfriend. My father was playing, they made eyes at each other, and so on. I knew the story, she knew I knew it, so I was prepared for a short piece of nostalgia, as a sort of nightcap.

"Your father was working bars and dance halls then," my mother began. "Once or twice a night club.

"This was when we were going together. I used to come watch him play, sometimes with a girlfriend, but then more and more often alone. They were pretty rough, some of the places. I used not to get very much sleep, out at nights and working during the days. And I used to get in trouble at home, though not too much since I was after all twenty and paying my board. I loved your father. He was a good singer, too, so natural — you could tell he loved doing it. So was the rest of the band good, much better musicians than your father, but not singing. Anyway, this guy saw them play one night. He wanted them to go out on the road.

"We were pretty serious then, your father and I. We

wanted to get married. And he was good, but he wasn't that good. The rest of the guys were real hepped-up on this road thing, but he kept putting them off for as long as he could. We didn't want to be separated for that long.

"One day my dad heard about this good deal on a little brick farm house, just on the edge of town. He was a carpenter by trade, so he heard about deals when they came up. I already knew Dad had a couple of hundred dollars he was keeping for a wedding present, if and when. I asked and he said we could use it as a down payment, if we wanted, and if we kept the wedding small.

"It took a couple of days for me to decide, but then I did and I went and told your father. I told him we could get the house if we moved fast — then I told him Dad and I had had a fight. He wasn't going to let me marry some guy who was out on the road all the time, doing God knew what in the hotels every night. I told your father that we could get married and get the house, but only if he quit the band. It was a condition, like it was coming from my dad. So he did."

She paused here and I thought she was finished. I didn't know what to say.

"The other guys, they were getting tired of waiting anyways. He would have had to quit soon, on his own. I mean, he was good, but he wasn't that good. And it's not easy, living on the road, no home. There wasn't much else for a woman in those days — secretary, cashier, a blank wall after that.

"So then we moved in here." She swept her hand over the brick-patterned tablecloth to indicate the tiny house I'd grown up in. Then she tipped her glass up to swallow the last of her drink. Again I thought she was finished.

"And here I am at my age. Learning how to run a bloody sander, for a boat that never will get out of that freezing basement of his." She laughed, hesitantly. Still I didn't respond.

"He must have found out. He talked to Dad all the time. Never said anything, though. All those years, selling, on the road..." She seemed to want something from me. She seemed to be losing the thread of what she was saying. I was tired and drunk and I didn't know what to say to this, a small dishonesty from so long ago that it couldn't matter. I tried to force a laugh, but it wouldn't come. Then it was as though she decided she'd waited for me long enough. She stood up, a little drunkenly, even angrily, pushing the table away from her and against me, the tablecloth bunching just below my chest. I thought it was a signal that the evening was over and she was about to head for her room.

"You know," she said softly, leaning her large hands on the table, "he called for you at the end. Always blamed himself for the trouble you got in, for you staying away all those years. Used to cry sometimes, at the end, saying he never could do anything right."

I suddenly felt ill. I tried to stand up, but with my knees jammed between table legs and the cloth threatening to slip off and send things flying, I couldn't very easily. My mother walked over and put a hand on my shoulder.

"But it doesn't matter." She looked away, studying, it seemed, a spot on the wall, before continuing. "A novel, eh? That's just a big story, isn't it?" She laughed a little, hoarsely, not expecting an answer. With her free hand she adjusted the cardigan around her shoulders.

"It's cold," she said. "Cold and damp."

Other Women

Oct. 1

There is a crisis at the clothes closet this morning. Standing in front of it, Muriel's feet are cold against the hardwood floor. She raises up and down on her toes, as though this might help. As she does, two small rolls of belly fat jiggle against each other within the fine net of her panty-hose; she punishes them with a couple of thumps of her fist. She notices her coffee cooling on the make-up table, and finally her feet will stand no further indecision: she pulls a loose flowered blouse from its hanger in the closet.

Now that Muriel has started, she moves quickly. She pulls the blouse on over her head, and tries not to notice the washed-out grey colour of her bra when she straightens her collar. She pulls on rumpled slacks from the bedside chair and is only briefly thankful for the nylons which protect her skin from the cool, damp material. She slips her feet into a pair of casual suede shoes, worn now so that she needn't bother with untying and retying laces. At the make-up table, the grey roots of her hair do not bother her as they had the night before, and she is deft with a few carefully pre-decided cosmetics: eye-liner applied light-handedly, neutral lipstick and eye-shadow; her hand passes directly over her favourite perfume to a light cologne, and she shares out a single finger dab between two earlobes.

But it's been done, hasn't it? The same situation, same words, same character. Housewife, mother, woman oppressed by husband, children, society. The whole thing is a bit ... well, it's a bit cliché. *Right?*

Right? Like he wasn't going to be satisfied until I gave in and said uncle to his declaration.

Right? Right?

Right. Yes, Christo*pher*, right. Aunt.

So the stuff of my last story was a little familiar, alright, very familiar, similar to a novel I'd read only *after* I'd started the story. And so the idea for this one isn't much more original. So what? So am I an old story, familiar: middle-aged woman dusting off old B.A. and heading off to graduate school. But so is he for that matter, perspicacious chap that he thinks he is, a Poet capital P, like most of the others in the class: rebels doing guerilla warfare against the tyranny of grammar. He, would-be hippie, yearning for a decade he was too young for — he told me himself. Writing his little egotistical, self-indulgent poems. Handing down his literary judgements from on high. Christ, I've lost more books on buses than he has ever read.

How childish. I embarrass myself even as I write such things, even here in my most solitary of places, my journal. But that's what it's for, isn't it? To embarrass oneself, get it all out of the system so it doesn't slip in and taint the important work. (*The important work.* How many times must Chris have written that in private to have said it to me so casually?) We discussed it once over coffee, journals, diarists, agreeing that much of Nin's diaries, written to be published, were self-aggrandizing, self-justifying, so much posturing; arrogant and fraudulent.

So he was right, though bumbling, tactless, back in those first few classes of the year. We've had a couple of coffees together since, me paying since his funds for the term have been somehow held up. And at least he doesn't treat me like somebody's mother. Not like the girls, women — Jesus, what about the tyranny of so-called liberation? For they are girls, that *is* the word; so many of them, too, in the department — young women, then. Although I know they wouldn't like that either, would think I was patronizing. When in fact I was the one condescended to, at first. Then resented, a representative of their own mothers sent to keep an eye on them.

Digression, infinite digression. Always I'm losing the point. Sometimes I think my life has been lived on a tangent.

Forget it, this. I'm becoming paranoid, a menopausal wreck quaking in her Wallabys. Probably they don't think of me at all, my colleagues. (Back again. I am a tenacious tangent treader, at least.) Probably it is simply me transferring what I fear Elizabeth thinks onto them, those other women's children. And even these fears are not true, I know. Hasn't it been *she* who rings *me* to meet on campus for coffee this last month? *She* who deflated all my carefully planned self-justifications the evening I broke to her the news that I might return to school, her school? It was just fine with her. That was that. We spent the rest of the evening discussing the relative merits of medical schools she might attend, a pain in my stomach throughout from unexpended emotion.

So it is me, all me. Constructing the emotional lives of others in my own mind — a symptom, no doubt, of imagination gone to seed, wasted on self-defeating fantasy. At forty-four I should by now have learned that it is useless to try to predict the feelings of others. You can never know for certain. Never can you count on them to feel anger, or guilt, or even love when they should. And even when they lay claim to one of these, there is no proof, how do you know? Do they even know? Sometimes I think that all the emotional relationships I have ever had have been fantasies, I have been wrong so often; that my life is a dream of imagined resentments, loves, communications, all of it lived from this terrible solitary control centre, me. For where is the record of emotion? Everything can be put to the lie, denied at some later date. What proof is there ever of a hand squeezed beneath the sheets before sleep, or a breast gently cupped; and where is it notarized that these things must be love, could not happen with a stranger, or do not cover some other feeling? Do you love me do you love me do you love me? Yes yes yes, we've signed up haven't we, declared, and everybody knows anyway that these things are transient, not like a lifelong subscription to some magazine — or even if it were, you could hate somebody while you loved, the hate cancelling out the other.

And yet there are some things which I do know, which must be certain. Like Dennis screaming his love at Elizabeth when she was going through that bad stage in early adolescence — acts of negative love. The third time in my life I have seen him cry, afterwards. Yes, there are some things which I do know for certain; and although I have been proved wrong other times, always it seems that these others were never as certain as the rest I still know, that there was always some essential difference.

Yes, it is in these small things that we know: the squeezed hand, the family squabble.

And so we live our clichés in our attempts to be ourselves. With monotony now, I wear my slacks and baggy shirts. I am not allowed denim jeans else the cold rays of silent disapproval zap me from within and without: old woman trying to be young. Nor can I wear my tweed suits for fear of appearing to copy the few women professors here. I gotta be me, you gotta be you, and a straight and narrow life it is. Never mind that my wardrobe leans heavily towards the wooly styles I have been forced to abandon, or that Elizabeth and I have been exchanging clothes since she was sixteen.

Other Women

Oct. 5

Feminism. And neither am I allowed to discuss feminism. The women here all know it already, it is history, required reading for some undergraduate course taken long ago. So what that a reasonably attractive woman can still buy a grade for sex, or that the oppressed women I tried once to write about, albeit poorly, still exist. It is considered bad taste or impertinence to bring it up.

Chris seems the only one willing to discuss such matters — which is why, I suppose, it came up in the first place with the others. For the past three days running the two of us have been having coffee together at the Grad Society. He is quite well-informed, quotes Plath and Adrienne Rich to back him up (I'd barely read the first, never heard of the second); he likes Greer for some sound reasons and I've been forced to re-evaluate her.

Oct. 8

I drove to London, Ont. today with Chris and two others from the writing class, Debra and Cynthia. Debra is in fact the way Cynthia's name implies she might be: stiff and formidably well turned out, Bay Street secretary with a slight case of rigor mortis. Cynthia is neo-sixties: ragged jeans, Indian shirt, a Chinese-style quilted jacket. Both write the sort of poetry you might expect from their clothes.

It was Chris's idea to go. Three poets were to give a reading he wanted to hear, and to hear him tell it, London, a two-hour journey, seemed only a couple of blocks down the street.

The poets, when we finally heard them, were disappointing, ranging from poor to mediocre in the opinion of all. Chris did an unusual thing before we left to return home: he took me aside and borrowed two dollars. He has been very scrupulous about even accepting a coffee on me until his money comes in and he is in a position to repay. Besides, there was no place around for him to spend it that I could see. Later, out on the highway as we approached home, he made a great show of presenting the money to me for gas. A small disturbance in the back seat followed: Cynthia passed forward a dollar and sixty-three cents; Debra, more reluctantly, a neatly folded dollar. I gave Cynthia back the sixty-three cents. Chris slouched in the passenger seat, his arms folded over his belly; he seemed to find the passing landscape somehow amusing.

Oct. 12

Today is Sunday. This morning Dennis and I made slow, beautiful love. For a time my breasts were firm, and my thighs were no longer webbed by those small, hateful, blue veins. Dennis rediscovered that small responsive spot at the small of my back, and for an hour we were both delighted by it. Later, tonight, we will go to the film theatre to see one of those art movies which Dennis really dislikes, yet is so skillful at analysing and understanding.

We have been close today, and therefore able to discuss those things close to us. We talked about Elizabeth and how, despite what we might have wished, she has become typical of her generation — conservative, cynical, material-minded and ultimately narcissistic. We were on dangerous ground here, for Dennis's success in advertising, especially lately, is light years from what any of us foresaw at his long-ago graduation with a degree in Philosophy. For a moment we almost talked about that since, for as long as I can remember, he has flirted with the idea of quitting. But the moment passed, and we continued to talk of our child. Fresh from sex ourselves, we wondered about her sex life. When she was young, when she still lived with us, she never seemed to concern herself greatly with boys, which saved us a worry then which we decided in retrospect might have been better to have. She has had her own place near the university for the last three years, and we are sure she must have some kind of sex life; she does not have that bundled, musty air about her which virgins, especially in academe, seem so early to acquire. Still though, knowing our daughter, so suited for the starched white lab coats she wears, it is hard to imagine her as anything but frigid (though from experience with other women friends, I know externals can deceive). In a moment of whimsey we imagined her initiation into the sexual world: panting, bespectacled Chemistry student growing quite frenzied atop (beneath?) our stiffened daughter, frantically dipping into, trying out, and discarding the materials in his limited sexual bag of tricks. I told Dennis how I imagined our own Liz quite excited by the experiment — running afterwards, slide in hand, to her microscope for a closer examination of her first live spermatozoon. We laughed — it was much funnier than it sounds here — and somehow ended up back in the bedroom ourselves. Perverse, I know, becoming aroused by the sexual possibilities of one's own children.

Oct. 16

It's got to be quite a habit, Chris and I going for coffees before classes. We have long talks about literature. We seem to complement each other's ignorances: he knows little or has forgotten most of what he did know about pre-twentieth century literature other than Shakespeare and the Romantic Poets; I know little about poetry, especially contemporary poetry. He has turned out to be quite a good critic of my own writing, I was surprised. And I, with my more traditional background, have made some comments on his work which he seems to have found useful. It is an odd situation. I, with the host of unliberated tendencies I continually find in myself, tend to defer to him since he is a man; but he is almost as young as Elizabeth, and at times I yearn to brush the too-long hair from his eyes as we talk. And yes, too, I harbour a secret desire to feed him, for he is as thin as all his generation seems to be. Lately, I have admitted some of this to him. Now we alternately fight such things as they come up and laugh about them. As I think I have mentioned before, he has never treated me like somebody's mother. I don't know what his own mother, either of his parents, is like, just that he never mentions them or seems to see them.

Oct. 22

It's been Indian Summer out these last few days. God, beautiful weather. I have stories, ideas for stories, coming out my ears. Not for here, though. That is another part of my life.

Oct. 24

Today I introduced Chris and Elizabeth. It seemed only natural that I should have them meet, I like them both. I wasn't sure if Elizabeth would like Chris, she has that priggish side to her. But also (I'll have to tell him about it later) it was a good chance to get some food into Chris — a mother is always allowed to spring for lunch for her daughter, and any company can hardly object to a parental picking-up of the whole check.

We arranged to meet at Amillio's, just off campus. An amazing thing. They seemed to hit it off from the very beginning, Elizabeth laughing, losing control even of the corners of her mouth sometimes, Chris wittier than I have seen him, talking about some comical character in the Graduate Society whom they both seemed to know. That was at the beginning, through salad, say. After that, they seemed to try to control themselves more, as if they were liking each other too much in my presence. Or no, were politely trying to include me. Chris asked of the waitress, "Are there wives in the avocados, babies in the tomatoes? And who did kill the pork chops anyway?" which was all an allusion to Ginsberg for my benefit — I only knew it since he'd quoted the lines to me himself, before. Elizabeth smiled through the rest of dinner, but I could see the corners of her mouth were in control again. Still, the rest of the time went quite well. It is dangerous to have too much hilarity over spaghetti. We were all enjoying ourselves by the end, chewing on leftover garlic bread, satisfied with the meal and each other. In an excess of generosity, which no doubt was compensation for less desirable feelings shortly before, I invited them both to come out to the house for supper one night. They both thought it a good idea, and set about deciding a day. It turned out the earliest convenient day for all is next Tuesday. Today is Thursday.

Nov. 26

It is cold in the house tonight. The furnace has been acting up again. Dennis is in one of his quiet, sullen moods, and I don't feel I have the energy to extract the cause from him so he might be relieved.

Met Chris and Elizabeth for coffee today at the Graduate Society. Irrational, yes, but I resented the fact that she was there. She is an undergraduate yet, and it is not her place. It belongs to Chris and to me, and to all the others who have struggled through their four years for the right. Granted, she was Chris's guest, and she is almost there, fourth year in that frightening and bleak field (to me), microbiology.

But it went alright. None of us felt too constrained, though we have barely seen each other these last few weeks. Chris and I got into quite a discussion about who and what poetry should be for — a bit more general than most of our

THE SAD EYE

talks, and somehow that seemed significant. Elizabeth sat back, very proper in her guest's position, asking a few educated layman's questions during the lulls to show her interest. She seems quite glad that Chris and I still seem to get on so well, though it is hard to tell — her face doesn't move; she has the most inexpressive face I have ever known, always withholding, impenetrable. She is in the wrong field, I know; she needs more concern with the larger organisms in life, I have always thought. Something to soften her. When I suggested years ago that she might consider the Arts or Humanities in university, I had poor reasons to back me up. If I had the suggestion to make today, I would mention her face.

Dec. 3, morning

Last night in bed, it was Dennis who actually mentioned what had already occurred to me several times. Chris is quite sexually active judging by his poems, which are often of a confessional nature. Dennis wondered when the first poems involving Elizabeth would start showing up in Chris's and my class.

Dec. 9

A slew of papers due these last few weeks, so I haven't had time for this. Two stories recently polished up and finished, one of childhood, one a wild parodic piece set in a seaside resort in the south of France. Both well received by the class; they granted the parodic nature of the second without my even having to argue for it. Glancing up at my last entry I can say that, at least for the present, Elizabeth's virtue will not be held up for public scrutiny — Chris has taken to using a persona in his latest poems, a young girl, and he claims to have a whole cycle in the works. They are quite good from what I can tell.

Other Women

Dec. 10

Have just put the finishing touches to one last paper. One manuscript to finish typing and I'll be done for hols. Xmas shopping to consider next. God, how I dread Xmas.

Later

The paper I have just finished today is on authorial intrusion in George Eliot. I ruffle the pages of this notebook and I know there are not things in it which should be. I spend long seconds poising my pen. I have not intruded my own self here enough — a cryptic statement, suitable for diaries. Full of deep meanings.

Later

Dreading Xmas. They will be over then, of course. There is no chance Chris will return to that wilderness town in the north from which he sprang.

I know how it will be. Chris and Elizabeth will come over around two on Xmas day, after having spent the best part of the day together. They will enter burdened with gifts, with overcoats; there will be a scuffle at the door — too many people stamping feet, well-wishing, relieving each other of objects. We will move en masse through the kitchen, picking up drinks, loudly anticipating the turkey which will be cooking in the oven, sampling exposed goodies. It will be a slow process which finally brings us to the living-room; our group will disintegrate around the various kitchen activities, and we will straggle in. It will happen then, or at some other time during the day, that each of us will be alone for a moment with the Xmas tree, and for that moment it will embarrass us slightly — this child's thing among grown-ups.

But that will be just for a moment, sometime. For after

the kitchen, we will give gifts, and we will eat the meal I will have prepared; and there will be great admiration of both. Afterwards, we will have coffee and dessert in the living-room. Dennis will sit in his easy chair, warm and good-spirited from the meal and the season. The children will no doubt sit together on the couch; Elizabeth will be chatty, her face active, happy, for she will be in love or well on her way. Full already, Chris and Elizabeth will pick through the confections on the coffee table in front of them — fudge, cookies, cakes — discovering delights for each other.

No, there will be no opportunity for that low hoarse voice she can sometimes use, that set face. The situation will not arise.

But it will be re-created, won't it? The events-leading-up-to pointing like a finger. Right?

I have just flipped back, and no, it isn't here. I could have been chronicling the weather. *To embarrass oneself.*

I should really change the date here. What was it? Oct.... 30? 31? Hallowe'en? Ha!

What was it we ate that night? It was a roast, something easy, yet which neither of them was likely to have had otherwise.

I remember how it was before they came. Dennis and I were in the kitchen. The room was warm, hearth-like from the oven. Dennis had come in shortly before and was in a good mood. He sat at the kitchen table, flushed from the heat and from drinking at some office celebration he'd been participating in — he told me all about it, but that is all I remember, the telling, his voice warm and familiar as our kitchen while I worked. He opened the bottle of wine we were to have with our dinner and poured out large glasses of it for both of us. I was thirsty from the cooking, drank mine almost immediately, and had a second. We talked at the table for a few minutes, he infecting me with his mood, more communion than communication. Then I gave him the potatoes to mash, and went to the kitchen sink to wash up a few dirty dishes which we would need for the meal.

I remember me there, of course. I was wearing my loose cooking shirt, bra-less for the heat. Dennis hadn't noticed, or hadn't thought anything of it. I could see his reflection in the window over the sink. As I washed, watching, listening, it seemed like I could *feel* the sound of his voice; it, the hum of running water, became like vibrations within my own body. I began to feel quite the sensualist. I took sips of wine between each dish that I washed; I grew playful with the billows of suds sitting so lightly on my skin, the glass. I finally became more and more conscious of the weight of my breasts against the fabric of my shirt; they seemed somehow to sway beneath my clothes of their own accord, warm and moist from the steamy dishwater.

Then *they* came in: a few token raps, a rush of cool air, and there they were together, standing on our kitchen floor. We ate almost immediately, since everything was ready. Dennis opened a second bottle of wine.

The meal went well enough, I can say that. Dennis was witty under the influence of so much drink, and Chris, under the influence of Elizabeth, rose to meet him. The two seemed to share political views and traded remarks about current policies and politicians, and finally about esoteric political theory, which all soon left me behind. Elizabeth, though, apathetic about such things for as long as I can remember, seemed to have become politicized; she suddenly was knowledgeable about such things as socialized medicine, the uses and misuses of subsidized drug plans, and even other issues far outside her immediate concerns. I thought it good that the three of them got on so well; I was busy bringing in and clearing off dishes, and keeping the wine glasses full. Afterwards, we went into the living-room and I brought in pie and coffee.

The talk became more general after that. Gradually, Chris and I seemed to become more in tune with each other, more like the two people who had shared so many coffees together. We told some stories of school, and described, for the benefit of Dennis and Elizabeth, some of the more eccentric characters in the department, freely embellishing as we went. Elizabeth, somehow infected by us, told an uncharacteristically comic story of the night the entire stock of rhesus monkeys was released from the research lab, somehow finding their way to the office of one of her more unlikeable instructors. The time seemed to pass quite quickly. Finally Dennis, perhaps reminded of his own school days by our talk, brought out a few of his by now well-polished anecdotes having to do with philosophers ancient and modern — telling how the Cynics got their name and such. Chris seemed to find them amusing, and even Elizabeth, who must have heard them nearly as many times as I. We'd long finished coffee by then, as well as the rest of the wine from supper and a part bottle I'd discovered in the refrigerator. As Dennis was talking I realized how very late it had grown and suggested we might all like some more coffee. We all did and I went into the kitchen to make it.

From the kitchen I could hear the voices in the other room, though not what they were saying. I felt quite gay, alone yet near the others. I found a half glass of wine that had been left behind and drank that. At the stove I took my time with the coffee, holding the measure high over the bowl in the percolator, and letting the grounds shower down into it. I felt some of my before-supper mood returning. I noticed I was still wearing my cooking shirt and was both surprised and proud that I hadn't been self-conscious about it. Still, I

Other Women

began to anticipate the departure of our two guests, and I wondered if perhaps Dennis was too.

When I entered the room the three of them were heatedly discussing politics again. I saw Dennis had brought out a bottle of French brandy which I didn't recall ever seeing before. He had poured some for Chris and himself, and for Elizabeth who, I know, has never liked it. For a moment I had a childish impulse to return to the kitchen and try entering again.

Instead, I walked in front of them, across the room to the endtable on the far side of Dennis's chair. I picked up a plate of cookies I'd placed there earlier when Dennis had declined pie. None of this seemed to disrupt their conversation at all. For a moment I just stood there, off to one side with the cookies, unsure of what to do with them now that I held the plate. Then I walked over to the couch. I bent over the coffee table to offer some to Chris and Elizabeth; since we'd all been drinking so much, I thought it might be a good idea for them to eat something. Chris took one absent-mindedly, ducking his head around me to maintain the line of conversation with Dennis; Elizabeth refused. I felt a little light-headed from the bending and it seemed a natural enough movement from standing there in front of them to seating myself on the arm of the couch next to Chris. I balanced there for a time listening half to the conversation, half for the coffee to perk.

Is this really necessary? Is it *really* necessary? Is there any reason why I must describe the rest — the bringing in of coffee, the overt flirting with Chris, the exposure of swaying cleavage as I served, like one of those vulgar blonde hostesses from a British bedroom farce? My pen slips through perspiring fingers as it is; my face radiates heat. What was it I wanted to record? Was it simply embarrassment?

Is it perhaps this: the moment of *shared* embarrassment, that of two people, their hands coming together, and a third as she backs away; that moment of common indictment: old woman trying to be young? Is that it? Is that right? Is that *all* this is about?

Dec. 11

A night of hard sleeping.

It is hard to believe now I ever wrote that drivel about there being no record of emotions. There are some things of which I will always have a record, I know now. The breast cupped, the family squabble. Acts of love, acts of negative love. Indelible. Indelible as the image of two hands coming together, as the knowledge of my daughter's tense, ungiving mouth. Indelible as the message from that silent mouth, indelibly reflected, though only for a moment at a nightmare dinner party, in another face.

But it is done. It has been done.

And the important work goes on.

The Sad Eye

It was during the summer I was fourteen that I almost became Artistic. That was the summer my father and Linda and I spent on Formentera, the southern-most island of the Balearic chain in the Spanish Mediterranean. My father was a potter — well known even then — and a friend had given him the use of a kiln and cottage/studio for a few months. Linda was a clothing designer, on a small scale, in Montreal, which was our home base then. But Linda wasn't working that summer. She needed a rest. As my father put it, she needed to "refresh the creative juices."

My father and Linda and most of their friends were, of course, already Artistic. The word to me, then, conveyed rather more than it generally does. It had to do, naturally, with things creative and with artistic talent; with the possession of imagination and with personal grace and style. But there were other things it involved. It suggested, among much else, body type; or perhaps more accurately, body tone.

My father had a peasant's body — so he described it. His shoulders were wide, his chest thick, his hands strong and stubby-fingered. He had a full red beard and reddish brown hair which he wore in a ponytail tied in two places. He's been described as a sculptor and ceramicist, but the term he used was potter. At our apartment in Montreal other artists often gathered in the evenings, slim and long-haired, most of them younger than my father, many of them francophone. This was in the second half of the sixties and my father did not speak French and was political in only a general way. Yet he would preside, making his pronouncements on art and life; and the young would put aside their natural arrogance, the real and would-be revolutionaries struggling with my father's English. Some, particularly the young women, literally sat at his feet, their shoulders and hair accessible to his fingers as clay. They would no more have argued with him, except as a rhetorical device to draw him out, than with a Rodin sculpture.

Linda was born in Sweden. She had fair hair, as long as my father's but finer. Unlike my father, she was small, lissome and virtually flat-chested. She and her partner employed three people in their shop and supplied several boutiques with their creations. She spoke both French and English fluently and was about twenty-six, more than ten years younger than my father. She was sometimes called upon during evening gatherings to interpret some point of aesthetics into French. Oddly, if there ever was any resentment it was directed at her, at these times, usually by one of the young Quebecois women. Twice I remember very heated exchanges in French, each with a different woman. Possibly they didn't like her accent or considered her art form a dubious one — I'm sure she made money at it — but that is beside the point. According to my definition, she was Artistic, at least as much as and probably more than the others.

I stood in contrast to Linda and these friends and my father. Sometimes I wondered how I could be my father's son at all. I was already taller than he, my hair dark brown and far shorter than I could have had it if I wished. And I was a fatty. I had no illusions that under the lard my father's musculature waited to be discovered. At school, I steered away from subjects my father and Linda might have approved of — art, music, literature and (instinctively, not logically) ath-

The Sad Eye

letics. I excelled at things like math and science. I couldn't have been less Artistic. With maybe one exception.

At night, at boarding schools and summer camps, and then later from ten on after my father married Linda, I had one particular pastime that in my own mind came to be associated with the Artistic way of being. Alone in bed I imagined countless flexing pictures of my mother. If I did not resemble my father and could not — didn't even by accident — resemble Linda, then I must take after my mother. The only solid fact I had was that my mother had been a painter and lived with my father in New York up until I was nearly four. I was curious to find out more about her, naturally, but not enough to break through my father's reluctance to say anything about her. And paradoxically, although I was curious I was also strangely satisfied with my own shifting idea of her. I had one other piece of information: that she was said to have committed suicide. This I knew from my own vague memories reinforced over the years by equally vague references. But I didn't consider it an absolute fact and never tried to find out details. Detail-less, bare, it was easier to deny or transform: my mother had left a note, went one of my stories, that she was going to drown herself in the Hudson; but her body was never recovered. Or this: the note again, and a burned body with her jewelry on it found after a fiery car crash; actually she had given the jewelry — she was a very generous woman — to a poor lady. In both cases she'd been stricken with amnesia. There were a number of other possibilities, not all of them so nice or naive or impossible. For instance: my father was lying. My mother was in an insane asylum, and my father wasn't telling me to spare my feelings. Or else he had committed her for reasons of his own.

During the year before Formentera my one Artistic activity was supplemented by, and oddly merged with, another. I started to have wet dreams; then wet fantasies. It would usually go like this. I would be imagining my mother and this would go on for the normal length of time. Then, from some dim control centre in the ganglia, I would get the signal it was time to switch over to, say, Magneline, the plumpish seamstress who worked for Linda. The most wonderful erection would present itself to my waiting hand — satiny and hard, and, yes, Artistic. I would stroke it, talk to it, usually of sexual matters but not always, and quickly or at length I would come.

My father sighed, tracing a thumbnail around the seed-shaped signature mark on one of the pieces a dealer had recently returned as unsaleable.

"You will like Formentera," he told me.

Even I could see why the series of vaguely anthropomorphized fruits and vegetables he'd made the year before hadn't been successful. Particularly the one he held, a ceramic eggplant on the earliest verge, it seemed, of transforming to a human skull.

"No I won't," I told him with, for me, unusual boldness. Maybe it was the yuckiness of the eggplant that gave me courage. But mostly it was because I was speaking from complete conviction.

For one thing, all my friends — the few I had, these slowly acquired — lived in Montreal. I had no desire to learn Spanish; as little as I had to learn French. The idea of having a sea at my disposal did little to tempt me. Overweight, I dreaded public exposure of my body. In fact, the reason I kept my hair so short — relative to my father's and at a time when most boys my age were battling long and hard each trip to the barber shop — was that some malicious school mate had accused me of having breasts. Not an entirely inaccurate accusation, I was doing my best to emphasize or at least make clear my gender. I had even embarked, contrary to

The Sad Eye

natural inclination, on a program of exercise that included a fair number of push-ups by the time the idea of the summer came up. So that was another thing. I didn't want to interrupt my regimen.

Since my father seemed, uncharacteristically, in an uncertain frame of mind, I must have taken advantage of it and mentioned one or two of these or other objections. But early in that short conversation he raised a point of his own. Linda needed a rest, he said. It was so undeniably true that I couldn't really answer it. Linda, a work horse for all her slightness of build, had actually been taking days off work, staying in bed, looking pale and drawn and enervated. My father responded by spending more and more late evenings at his studio, crosstown, which only made matters worse. At gatherings in our apartment — less frequent lately — Linda would sit by herself drinking large quantities of wine, excusing herself early, even before me, to go to bed. But for the sheer will of my father and an unprecedented, obviously unnatural heartiness on his part, she would have cast a pall over the whole of such proceedings. Linda and I were not close, and I was not the most observant fourteen-year-old, but even I could see something was wrong. The need for a rest was as good a name for it as anything.

The unsold fruit things were pulverized and put out with the garbage.

We went to Formentera.

And I was right — I didn't like it.

I didn't like the getting there to begin with. I was alternately nauseous and bored on the long plane rides that got us to Valencia; I was wretchedly sick on the ferry between Valencia and Ibiza, an eight-hour voyage that glued me to the deck railing within the first twenty minutes seaborne. My father had a difficult time persuading me even to board the other smaller ferry that left Ibiza for the little island of Formentera only an hour after we mercifully set foot on dry ground. My sole consolation was the thought that every miserable voyager in the history of the world has probably had: things would be alright once we finally got there.

But things weren't alright when we got there. It took more than a week before we settled in, a good seven days requiring much telephoning and transporting and day-tripping on my father's part to ensure that the crates and luggage following us arrived at their destination. By then I'd already become well acquainted with what became my chief torments for the summer: the heat, and a sort of corollary of it, the light. I'd learned that brilliance was a tangible thing you could feel like a metallic dust in your nose and mouth. I'd learned that the sun was an enemy, that it never quit and there were never clouds, and that these conditions were constants during that season on the island. And I'd formed the image which I carried with me for the next three months: of myself traversing the landscape and the face of the summer like a chunk of fat sizzling across a hot pan. It didn't help, I suppose, that I continued to wear then and for the rest of the summer my long-sleeved shirts — the only kind I owned — even with shorts. The long sleeves were meant to disguise the fact that my biceps were woefully underdeveloped for my age (my Montreal exercise program nipped, as it were, in the bud); the rest of the shirt, naturally, was necessary to cover up a general flabbiness. I didn't mind my legs.

Despite my original climate shock, I soon fell into a routine that summer. I liked routines.

I would rise in the mornings soon after my father. He would usually be sitting out on the rocks overlooking the water, naked to the waist, drinking a cup of coffee, picturesquely drawing whatever it was he drew by way of inspiration from the sea. Sometimes he was already in the work shed. In any case, I wouldn't disturb him. I would make myself breakfast — fried eggs and bananas with milk. Usually both, sometimes just one. I was used to having three meals a day from years of boarding school before Linda and my father married. I was used to cooking breakfast because neither Linda nor my father ate it, and neither was much of a cook even when they were around to try.

After this I would walk down along the shore. There was only one neighbouring cottage, I discovered after some long walks in both directions. This was a fairly large place for that island, more of a home than a cottage, with red-tiled roof, whitewashed cement walls and brightly flowering bushes here and there in the rocky, sea-facing yard. As near as I could tell the building was unoccupied. I don't know how precisely, but somehow I received the idea from my father that there was something wrong about the person who owned the place, possibly having to do with politics, and I was to stay away. It was to this property I would make my way most mornings. It wasn't the cottage that drew me; still less, interest in our absentee neighbour, wisely summering, I was sure, in more moderate climes. It was the trees.

In addition to the bushes there was a stand of five or six of these trees, broad-leafed and bugless, the only ones tall enough on our stretch of shoreline to offer any shade. They were a bushy species and closely grouped so that the ground in the midst of them, conveniently floored with soft, dry moss, formed a sort of nest, cool at that time of day. A few years earlier I might have called the spot a fort. Now I called it nothing, regularly wombing myself in after breakfast with enough necessities — lemonade bottle, fruit, book — to last for a few hours, and taking some satisfaction in violating my father's vague forbiddings.

I soon had the perfect spot hollowed out in this cave among the leaves, my back wearing smooth the bark of the broadest tree, food and drink placed an exact arm's length away, the hefty biography of Galileo I was reading that summer resting importantly on my knees. Here, in relative comfort, and in between snatches of Galileo's early life, I could nurse my preoccupations. I could watch the sun cruelly toying with my leaves; gaze balefully out at the relentless blue and glistening sea off to my right; recall the hoggishly spreading paraphernalia of my father's work back at the cottage; or gallantly pity Linda, left to her own devices in quest of the needed rest, what with my father working throughout the day and wobbling off on a bike, alone, to visit island friends at night. This — meaning the island, the whole of Spain, *everything* — this, I decided after due consideration, was *High* Artistic. I hated it all. And I knew — I even made a vow to that effect shortly after discovering my deciduous den — that nothing or no one, no momentary pleasure or passing diversion, would ever induce me to change my mind. No way. Fat chance.

Visiting the Spot (I did, eventually, have to call it something) was one of my two regular activities. The other took place later in the day.

There was a beach across the island where various hippie types gathered for swimming. It wasn't exactly a nude beach in the nearly institutionalized manner of such places in North America. But it was understood by that shifting island population that one could be topless — or, rather less frequently, bottomless — if that was what one was into.

I would ride my bike — we rented two for the whole summer — over to this area in the afternoons. It was a good half-hour trip over some hilly terrain and could turn into quite an ordeal, the towel tied to my handlebars invariably loosening and catching in the spokes, the bathing suit worn under my shorts riding higher and higher no matter how I tugged, chafing and binding and punishing me in an appropriate way for what I was setting out to do. It was not that I even planned to swim — I simply needed the trappings of bathing to justify my being there. My one other piece of gear was a pair of dark glasses, worn partially in hopes of disguise, more practically in order to see without being seen to see, but mainly, simply, against the incessant glare.

There was a slight rise overlooking the beach and I would pause here, damp and winded, to scout out the scene. There were usually more men than women, but it never occurred to me they might be doing the same thing as I. From this vantage point I would try to anticipate the most likely spot to spend my afternoon — an important choice, for once installed I felt committed to stay for the allotted time and would not allow myself to move for fear of anyone guessing what I was up to.

From here, trying to appear as casual as possible, I would coast my way down through the laid-out bodies to the selected site. I would lay my bike down, detach my towel, spread it, and with a high degree of diffidence remove my shorts to reveal my bathing suit. I would lie face down on the hot white rocks. So far so good, but I then faced the problem of removing my shirt in this awkward position. It took me several visits before I learned to unbutton before lying, but even then it was a clumsy process, and if anybody was interested I must have presented a comic sight. But nobody was interested, so far as I could see through my green-tinted view of the world. If anybody had laughed or even looked curiously at me, I probably would never have returned.

Finally ensconced, with a dry mouth and scorching back, I could safely turn my attention to the "real" beach scene around me: thin girls, heavy girls, older women, French, German, American, British — hardly any Spanish, I think — swimming, walking, sunning; a few, as shy as I if I only realized, hugging their beach towels face down. The men I found far less interesting: shaggy, hard-bodied and confident; boring at best, too like the group who would gather in my father's house; and at their worst, when they would come too close or look my way, threatening. The women probably had as much or as little similarity to those of my experience as the men, but the important difference with them was that my father wasn't there. They were mine, in the sense that anything not my father's was mine. And they were strangers, although some of them were familiar from town and, conceivably, knew me. I suppose it wasn't so much that they were strangers as that I myself was, a visitor. There were even children there, these the most likely to be completely naked, but fortunately they were very young. There was nobody my age, and that was how I liked it. I could picture any of this group despising me or telling me to get lost, but at least no one was likely to shout *look at those tits!* — meaning mine — even though I was shouting, or anyway thinking, similar words about some of them.

Of course during the high points of my watching I had such an erection it would have taken fire or flood to have got me to stand up in the presence of these people. I amend that to only flood, for twice during the first weeks my back got so burned it blistered, and feeling the prickles and itches even while it smouldered I hadn't moved until my time was up and I was in a decent state to do so.

Although I was fascinated by the beach nudity that summer, as any North American boy would be, I was probably more familiar with nakedness than most children. We, or rather they, were not a shy household in that regard. Almost against my will I knew intimately every hair and mole and wrinkle on my father's sea-god torso — particularly that summer, when, styling himself on who knows what bohemian vision, he seldom donned a shirt, except when he went out socializing at night, and then not always. More significantly, though, Linda had always had the clothing industry's impersonal attitude to bodies — including her own — that they are, basically, manikins, skeletons for the flesh of fashion. As long as I had known her she would walk around our apartment in various states of nakedness when dressing, almost always with panties on, but very often that would be all. Aside from a small shock the first time I had seen this, I had fairly well adopted her own attitude towards her body and I had a critical but non-erotic appreciation of it. That is why, when my father said simply that Linda needed a rest, I had understood immediately. The physical signs of weariness had been evident to me for some time, perhaps before even my father.

That summer I began to see other aspects of the physical Linda that I hadn't known about before.

For one thing she sweated. Even more than I did. She was a sun-worshipper — perhaps all Scandinavians are, at least latently — and she spent long hours that summer lying out, exposed to that brutal Spanish sun. I would often see her, even though I had my own spot for what sunbathing I did. After only a few minutes stretched prone on her chaise lounge one could see tiny beads of sweat popping on her lip, her forehead, even her cheeks. Little parallel rivers of sweat would form in no time along the shallow valleys on either side of her breastbone. She never wore a top sunbathing and practically speaking didn't need one: she had a boy's body — a slim boy's. In the sweating department, however, Linda and I had much more in common than either of us had with my father. When working at the kiln, blacksmith-like and in the full blaze of the sun, my father only worked up a slight dampness; and at other times, despite what you might expect from such a big-bodied man, he hardly ever perspired.

The sun, however, did other things to Linda than encourage perspiration and an ever-deepening tan. She was drinking more and more liquor, mostly rum. I suppose I blame the sun because I myself considered it such a malignant force and there seemed an obvious correlation between Linda's huge fluid loss and the need to replace it, the beaded glass of rum and lemon being never far from her sun- and sweat-soaked hand. In any case, the two combined — the drinking and the sun — did a peculiar thing. The deepening tan made her look far healthier than she had during the preceding months, while the liquor made her appear, often, at peace with herself, carefree even. On the other hand, it seemed at times as though she were literally aging before me, as though that tepid rum were drawn from some sort of reverse fountain of youth. The deepening creases at her belly as she stood, a sandy pea-sized freckle on the back of one hand, incipient wrinkles at her underarms and neck, the tiny spread wings of permanent crowsfeet — all these, I would swear, were not there before the island. She was twenty-six; she could, and did more and more as the summer progressed, look ten years older.

In other ways I didn't get to know Linda any better than I had before, although inevitably, since my father was the only one with regular work to do, we spent time together. A couple of times a week Linda and I would take the two bikes and ride into Puerto La Sabina, the only town of any size, to buy groceries.

After our shopping we would stop at a café and have a drink. I would have *café con leche* — about the only Spanish words I learned that summer — and Linda too would have coffee, with a double brandy, sometimes two. We would usually sit for a half hour or so, careless of what the heat was doing to our purchases. I was not immune to the ego-building sensation of having an attractive woman sitting next to me in a public place, even if she was my stepmother. Sometimes people would come up to talk for a few minutes. The owner of our cottage was well known on the island and there was at that time a burgeoning artists' colony located there who knew of my father in his own right. I found out that Linda knew German, for she responded easily in that language to laboured questions put to her in German-accented

The Sad Eye

English. But people tended not to stay long, and perhaps it is true that artists have extra sensitivity, for it didn't take any of them long to see that Linda didn't want company.

Without being vain, I think I was the one exception. The two of us would maintain a quiet at such times as these. Linda would twirl her brandy glass — or rum glass, depending where we were — looking deeply, tragically into it; I would dwell in my world, anticipating island activities, such as they were, or soaking bittersweetly in my own sea of grievances. As I said, in some ways I didn't get to know Linda any better than before; I think it was because I was incurious that we got along as well as we did, maintaining a sort of brother/sister indifference to one another. We liked being around each other, while at the same time — I could see it was mutual — irritating one another. It was only later I decided that the reason for this was that we had so much in common, while not much liking in ourselves those common things. If I'd been less concerned with myself, it's possible I might have learned what was troubling her, helped her, become her friend. But I doubt it. She was already Artistic.

I was not entirely accurate when I suggested our only neighbouring residence remained unoccupied. Although there was no grass to speak of and the rest of the vegetation seemed to take care of itself, I did assume that someone, friend or caretaker, occasionally looked in on the place. And I soon found evidence to support this notion — curtains out of line from the day before, scuff marks on the verandah I hadn't noticed previously, that kind of thing.

I didn't think much of these signs at first. Perhaps it was the dryness of Galileo's early life, perhaps the influence of paperback thrillers I began to pilfer from Linda's large stock, but somehow as the summer progressed these signs seemed more ominous. The house itself attracted my attention more

THE SAD EYE

and more; and as it did I seemed to find more and more signs of occupancy — a cigarette butt that wasn't there before, a few stones overturned in the narrow driveway — but *too* few, almost as though they were a slip made by someone trying to leave behind no mark. I rummaged through my mind for information about the owner of the place — there had been some talk about the island and its inhabitants among my father and his friends back in Montreal but I had intentionally tried not to hear. I had some idea that the owner was a bachelor, Spanish, an academic; possibly a member of the aristocracy; a Basque, perhaps, a Spanish separatist. But I couldn't know that much, and I wasn't sure, I had to admit with some disgust, if I wasn't just making some of it up. But hadn't my father hinted at danger? There seemed no reason — this was Spain under Franco, after all — why political intrigues couldn't be being planned under cover of darkness. Really. Anarchists, communists. They would need guns, of course, and a place to cache them . . . the ground under my very bottom seemed rather hollow. Naturally there would be two or three raven-haired female guerillas, a smudge of black on their cheeks . . .

At this point I would usually turn to matters in hand. For it was in the mornings now that I took my one Artistic indulgence, at least the carnal part, stimulated by remembrance or anticipation of my afternoon beach, by full-breasted revolutionaries, by whatever, but still conjuring in my mind, when it came right down to it, images from Montreal. Member erect, that unblinking Spanish sun already burning through gaps in the leaves, a steamy if blurred Montreal body before me, the idea of surreptitious goings-on at the cottage would recede. Afterwards, cleaning myself up with a certain amount of self-reproach and a carefully rationed handful of leaves, I knew that, if I really believed, I could easily check my suspicions out at night; but by that point they always seemed hopelessly silly.

The Sad Eye

It was early one morning; I'd only just got myself settled properly in the Spot.

"Hello," the voice said. Although technically my bottom may have kept some contact with the mossy ground, the rest of me literally jumped a good couple of inches. Behind me, half concealed by tree limbs, a woman was standing. I wasn't sure where she'd come from — the ostensibly unoccupied house, around from the side of it, or possibly from some hiding place among the weeds and bushes. I couldn't think of anything to say. Then inspiration, probably adrenlin-induced, struck.

"*Non comprends*," I said, boldly, rolling on a shoulder to look at her. It wasn't bad; dim self-congratulations stirred in the back of my mind. Unfortunately, it started her jabbering in some foreign language, probably French, although having just blown a good tenth of my at-hand non-English vocabulary and being in any case still too startled to attend, I wasn't sure. She went on in this indecipherable vein for quite a few seconds and it gave me time, keeping my eyes constantly on her, to collect myself and realize I hadn't been caught at anything too disreputable — not, thank god, at the belly-dancing gyrations I used to make my navel wink and talk to me, another pastime recently taken up, nor in anything worse. I'd just been reading one of Linda's detective stories, which I managed to edge under Galileo. The incomprehension must finally have showed on my face, however.

"You live down the shore," she said in English, in a tone more statement than question. "You are Edgar's son?" this time more question than statement. Many of the things she said would have this duality to them, one or the other dominating.

I'd found some more of my voice by then, enough to admit that I was indeed my father's son. She'd called him Edgar, which I found a little strange. Edgar was his artist's name, his second given name. There was only one ancient gallery owner in Montreal who called him that, and one or two friends from the old days whom he seldom saw. Linda, and anyone else at all acquainted with him, called him Robert. But I supposed — during the short time it was possible to suppose this — it was something a person who knew him by reputation only might call him. And she was a foreigner to boot, with the same accent that the Germans Linda talked to had.

She talked some more in English, innocuous stuff about the weather, the niceness of my Spot. Then, amazingly, she asked if I wanted to come up to the cottage — the Conquistador's house is what I'd started calling it privately — for a coffee. Still buzzing with relief that I'd escaped observation at a more compromising moment, the invitation didn't surprise me. Besides, despite the accent, there was something familiar, reassuring, about her; if she was a guerilla, I was sure, she was a benign one. I agreed. At the very least I'd get to see the interior of the house.

Inside she told me to sit down while she got the coffee. I did sit, on a modern, sort of Scandinavian design chair which matched the rest of the furnishings in the room. It was an impressive place, in a subdued way, with many books in bookcases: most of them hardcover and fairly old, but some more brightly contemporary and even a few paperbacks. There was a large old map on the wall, a reproduction of the world as it was some centuries ago, the names in a foreign language, Spanish or perhaps Latin. There were some modern paintings on the wall, small oils and watercolours, and on the low square tables a few small sculptures, one in what looked to be bleached bone, a material I thought especially appropriate to the island.

My hostess returned with our coffee. I still hadn't said much to her and was too shy to have even looked at her properly. She soon had me at my ease though, chattering away in a nervous sort of manner, rising several times unex-

The Sad Eye

pectedly, obviously interested in me — which flattered me — but not in an intense way which would have made me uncomfortable. She bombarded me with information — not too much, but enough so that I had to pay attention and had no time for my own nervousness. I found out that the owner of the house was a Señor Santiago, from Pamplona, and that as I'd thought he was a member of an old and aristocratic family, mainly on his mother's side. I discovered that Claudette (that was her name) was from Munich, a poet and sometime teacher, her family longtime friends of the Santiagos. Claudette's grandmother was French, which explained her first name and, I supposed, her knowing the language. She said Señor Santiago had let her use the place as a *pied-à-terre* — I knew the expression, she told me — but that she mostly spent her days with others she knew on the island and Ibiza. In any case, her time in Spain was nearly over.

I was glad she didn't ask me about my father; people were always asking about him and I was tired of answering the same questions. She also didn't mention school, another subject I had no desire to go into. In fact, while making me feel I was the focus of her attention, she asked me few direct questions about myself, which was the way I liked it. I enjoyed sipping coffee and listening and feeling sophisticated in a sophisticated room, warm but not yet hot, sunny but not overbright with the light coming in from the side windows.

This changed after we'd talked for some time, the lighting. At some point during a natural lull in the conversation, she walked over to the curtains covering the long windows facing the sea. She drew them open, and stood at an angle, looking out to sea or along the shoreline towards our cottage, it was hard to say which. She stood that way — it could have been a pose, but I didn't think that then — for some time. I had yet to take a good look at her and it was now, her eyes safely elsewhere, that I did.

She was a beautiful woman, there was no doubt of that.

But the sunlight — and she was standing in the full brilliance of it there at the window — made her something far beyond that. The sunlight was clearly her friend as the heat was my father's and as both were my enemy that summer. Its most spectacular effect was on her hair, and I realized then that there was a lot of it, in unexpected places.

The sunlight picked up and made goldenly translucent the long straight hairs on her legs — which were deeply tanned, no strangers themselves to sunlight.

Moving up and lingering long — but oh, never long enough — there was a ferny silhouette at the juncture of legs, mysterious, bidding.

Turned slightly sideways to me, that light, like a hard but amorphous animal, nuzzled shadow at her armpits, the surprising tawny wisps there languid, glistening damp.

And of course there was the long blond hair falling over her face, single pale filaments escaping here and there, the slight tangles prisming a mist of gold and light around her head.

If it sounds as though Claudette were naked, it was just about true. She wore a white cotton dress that was virtually transparent in the sunlight. She was thin-limbed, but heavy-breasted, and through the dress I could see small chocolate nipples, whitely veiled.

I don't know why all my vague summer-long erotic stirrings finally found an object and focus during those precise moments, during my quite consciously cinematic appraisal of Claudette. Maybe they would have attached to someone, anyone, within regular eyeshot, eventually, perhaps one of the recurring figures at the beach or even Linda, who was after all no blood relation. Up until then, though, they were still ultimately directed to increasingly dimly remembered pictures of Magneline and a few school girls I had known, this stubbornness tied in somehow with my rebellion against the island.

The Sad Eye

At any rate, by the time Claudette turned back from the window, I had a full-blown erection, mercifully restrained somewhat by the bathing suit beneath my shorts. I pulled the front of my shirt over this embarrassment as far as I could.

She walked to the side of my chair, talking again, now about the history of the island.

"Did you know the ancient Carthaginians back in, oh, before Christ, would bring their dead to these islands..."

I didn't know this or several other facts she told me, as she stood there a bare foot and a half away from my left arm and at a difficult angle to look at easily, but I did know the return of her deep conversational voice was helping to relax the straining tension of my cock, which moments before I'd feared would rip right through my sea-salt weakened clothing. Her tone didn't change and she never paused as she unbuttoned the front of her dress and I watched — eyes wide and hard left — it slide out of sight. So much for relaxation.

"I'm going now to bathe in the sun," she said, "before the day is too hot. You would like to come?" I was unsure what to do with my eyes, or rather unsure if it was permissible to do what I wanted to. I could see her large, round breasts from where I sat, and her nipples, smaller than any I had ever seen before, and I had seen quite a few that summer. They were erect, those nipples, and reminded me instantly of Rosebuds, a milk chocolate confection I had eaten often in Montreal. I couldn't see below her waist from that angle and I wasn't sure whether she had on the bottom of a bathing suit — I could have been wrong about the ferny juncture — and intended to bathe, like Linda, topless, or if I was meant to keep my head politely turned while she put on some sort of suit.

She moved a bit more around the side of my chair into view and glanced, so it seemed, at my crotch buried in its layers of clothing. "You would like to come," she said again and touched my shoulder. Under slightly different circumstances I would have bolted for the door, or perhaps ejaculated into my bathing suit, or maybe simply turned into a blushing lump of passive resistance. But as it was I was taken again by those nipples, swaying so close to my face. I was taken by their size, their erectness — but most of all by their Rosebud-likeness. I had had more than my share of these — Rosebuds — those tiny, chocolate dollops ending in a tiny filament which even the most impatient, greedy tongue could melt away. In a way it made her just the smallest bit ridiculous, brought her down to a level at least within sight, and left me, however marginally, able to function.

You would like to come and she was moving in front of me, the nipples mesmerizing, the hand on my shoulder moving to join the other in undoing the buttons of my shirt. She kissed me and even though my eyes were wide I don't quite remember the process that got my bathing suit and shorts off and the two of us onto the floor. Somewhere along the way my hand found or was guided to one of those nipples, reassuring in its smallness and dried sea-salt texture. She orchestrated all activity from breast height down — I do know that — and at some point I was inside her, sliding in and out atop her. I lasted a much longer time than what might be expected, considering — perhaps twenty or so deep and near-bursting heaves. At the end of it, I lay for a few seconds on her and found, happily, that I was still wearing my shirt, as though I were in some intermediate stage of sunbathing.

I felt glorious for those few seconds, but this was ebbing away towards a desperate need to escape and uncertainty about how I was to do it.

"I must take my bath now," she asked. Before I could figure out whether she was requesting my permission, or whether she meant a real bath, a sun bath, or a swim, she added, "You will come tomorrow. At the same time. I have

The Sad Eye

something to give you?" And then she rose and walked away through a doorway, her bottom firm and brown as the rest of her.

I dressed, walked to the cottage, and, avoiding Linda, took off on my bike. I rode a long way, up through the hilly end of the island, the hardest going on a bike. I bought two bottles of pop at an isolated little café and found a lonely spot on the shore where I sat meditatively — in a pose borrowing much from my father — drinking them. I swam. Later, I doubled back towards the other end of the island where I bought a half dozen sweet rolls wrapped in newspaper, which I brought back in my carrier. I managed to secrete these in my bedroom without anybody seeing.

The next day I waited until I knew that my father and Linda were well immersed in their morning activities. Claudette was already out, sunbathing on the wooden deck attached to the house, when I got there. She had on the bottoms of a bathing suit but no top. She was lying face up on a lounge chair, and although it was very warm there was enough of a breeze blowing to lightly gooseflesh her breasts; and there in the centres, the tiny chocolate nipples.

Outdoor nudity was a more normal sight for me and I was able to retain my composure well enough to walk over to her and present the package of sweet rolls. She must have been expecting me, for there was a coffee pot beside her, an extra cup and small matching cream pitcher and sugar bowl. An extra chair had been set up and I sat down, poured coffee and ate sweet rolls with her. She seemed calmer, less wound up, less of that mildly disconcerting ambiguity in her sentences. We talked for some time, about me, about, I think, Galileo, about her and her poetry. She told me some more about the history of the local islands: the necropolis on Ibiza, Isla Ahorados, also known as "Isle of the hanged men," the ancient goddess Tanit, worshipped by the Punics, whoever they were; I decided to find out more on my own. I enjoyed the conversation even more than our activity of the day before — even while I was hoping for a repeat of it — for those minutes then had covered such a range of strong emotions that enjoyment, if it was there at all, was only a small mixed part.

After a while she stood, suddenly, saying: "I have something for you." My crotch leaped with anticipation and I started to rise, thinking we were moving into the house. But she indicated I was to wait for her there.

It was then — something about her gesture, the sudden turn away from me — that I got my first inkling I had had all I was going to get from her, at least sexually. During the five minutes or so she was inside, it first occurred to me that she'd been more distant than I might have expected, even while we had talked more; that while, in a way, she seemed more interested in me personally than the day before, it was almost a polite interest. Even, perhaps, condescending.

I was just chalking these thoughts up to paranoia when she came out again, wearing a cotton blouse. This was natural enough since the breeze had increased a little while we talked, keeping those nipples at fascinating attention, and some clouds, a rarity on that island, had one by one been passing the face of the sun, making it seem cooler than it really was.

She was carrying something, a man's shirt, neatly folded as it would have been when new, although I could see it was long from being that, was quite worn in fact.

"This is for your father," she said. "You will give it to him for me?" I could see her breasts shift towards me as she passed it over, but the material of her blouse was heavier and of a tighter weave than that of the dress she had worn the day before and the sun had gone behind another cloud. I looked at her face instead. I hadn't estimated her age before that, simply thought of her as a Woman, older, sophisticated, beautiful, if anything around Linda's age. Looking at her face, a flake of skin here and there on her brow, the slight puffiness beneath her eyes, I thought she might be even older than Linda, late twenties. Or no, early thirties; possibly as old as... well, say, thirty-four, thirty-five. But she backed away, and she became, again, what she had been. "I must go bathing," she said. "And then I must go..." She walked back into the house and I followed her with my eyes, thinking she hadn't finished the last sentence, was momentarily stalled over some English word. When she didn't come back in a few minutes I realized she had finished, said all she had to say to me.

Walking back to our cottage, I made no special attempt to evade Linda, who was lying face down on a lounge chair near our back door, the first rum and lemon of the day by her on the ground. I walked very slowly, studying the offering or gift or whatever it was, as though I might get some explanations from it. It was a flannel shirt, probably long-sleeved, checked; it was tied with some coarse twine, looked clean but vaguely old-fashioned. It was inappropriately heavy for that climate, in any case, and I was just beginning to think it must be some sort of unorthodox wrapping for something else and to squeeze it to see if this was the case, when Linda raised her head and looked at me. She looked, raised her head even farther, and held that uncomfortable turtle pose for several seconds. Then she stood right up, and I realized she was not looking at me at all, but beyond me. I followed her gaze, looking back down the shore in the direction I had come from. Linda's hands, I'd noticed, were hanging limp by her sides, the one with the age spot turned towards me.

Looking back I could see Claudette standing at the water line, looking towards us. She had her hands on her hips and was wearing a bath robe now. I turned back to Linda who was now staring at what I held.

My father walked out of the house at that moment carrying some brushes. He couldn't see Claudette from that angle, but he could see the two of us and he must have realized something was wrong. He walked over. All three of us turned to watch Claudette.

This must have been what she was waiting for, or something like it. I watched, not close enough to see small details, as she let the robe slide to her feet. She entered the water and when she was in it up to her waist — she was completely naked — she started swimming straight out, her strokes long and clean. After she was out a good long way, she changed course and followed the shoreline away from us. Perhaps, I thought, she had arranged for the Conquistador to pick her up.

Eventually she was out of the scene, too far away to remain the focus for the three of us. We stood around in uncomfortable silence. I found the shirt in my hands. "This is for you," I said to my father. I turned away from the two of them, but not fast enough not to see the tears in Linda's eyes. I went inside, Linda's strained, accusatory voice starting up dimly behind me as I passed through the door. I made myself a second — third, counting the sweet buns — breakfast. I ate this and wandered around inside the cottage for a while and tried to read a mystery novel. Linda and I were supposed to be going shopping later that morning but I doubted if we would go now.

Just before noon I went outside again. Linda was gone, one of the bicycles missing. The sea looked bleakly bright before me, the sun having regained control of the sky. I could feel perspiration running in tracks down my sides. I decided then and there that we were going home. I would scheme, throw tantrums, injure myself, do something, anything, to make my father take us. I would approach it rationally, like a problem, a project. That would be my aim in life, until I realized it.

I went to the work shed, a place I'd never been that summer.

The Sad Eye

Inside it was hellishly hot, the kiln adjoining the building having been fired up. My father had been firing some work, very conventional things, pots and dishes and cups, which he'd been commissioned at an exorbitant rate to do. He had part of this project in front of him now, already fired but not yet glazed. There were some paints mixed next to him and some brushes. He was preparing to put on the Sad Eye.

I guess I will have to explain about the Sad Eye, although people familiar with my father's work might guess what I mean. My father always signed his work, still does, both with initials and with a mark. The mark was always an oval, although it could appear anywhere on a piece and varied enormously, from a little dab of paint, to an ostrich egg-sized thing with complicated and sometimes beautiful designs within. Much has been written by critics during my father's career about this mark, some of it wildly speculative and not all of it in praise, especially when it appears in its largest and arguably most unharmonious form on sculptures. I suspect I am the one person in the world who knows the truth about that mark, besides my father. I'd known for a couple of years and he knew I knew, and it was perhaps our one closeness because we'd never talked about it and therefore spoiled it by mutual discomfort or false sentiment. I knew because, during one of the perhaps half dozen times I'd been present while my father worked, I'd watched him applying the device without his knowing I'd seen. There'd been a look of such sorrow in his eyes, before he was aware of me and while his hand was making its delicate artist's movements, that I had known with a child's unerring certainty about such things not only that the look was genuine but to what it referred. The Sad Eye, as I called it, was my father's tribute — appropriately, painted — to my mother.

When I entered the shack my father had a tiny clean paint brush in his hand and was seated, the domestic items from the commission before him, preparatory to painting the Sad

Eye. Immediately I softened towards him, he with his ridiculous ponytail and clay-streaked beard and the hair on his wide bare chest frizzled as though singed. But then I noticed the shirt, tossed carelessly on a bench. I don't know what I planned to say, before I walked in there, but now I said this:

"She was a friend of yours." Was I asking him or telling him? He glanced up at me.

"I knew her a long time ago, Bobby," he said. "She reappears . . ." He tailed off and wasn't going to continue, I could see.

"She would be about thirty," I said, again that tone. He was studying the underside of a plate.

"She is crazy and spiteful and a fascist. She is a not-very-good poet, even in German," he said without raising his head.

"She speaks English very well."

"That is because she studied in America . . ." He looked up, and I could see his brain working, wondering just how much I had talked to her, to know how well she spoke English and to get so much of her in my voice.

"She would be, maybe, thirty-four?" Very briefly that sadness, that I had seen only one other time, passed through his eyes.

"Your mother is dead, son," he said, slowly and softly. My eyes felt water-logged, overweight with tears, but I wasn't crying, unless it was through my very pores — my shirt was sodden by now and beads of sweat ran steadily down my face. I'd known what he told me was true even before he said it; known it in a way I never had before.

"But she would have been in . . . America, New York, about the same time."

"No," he said, and I knew this was also true, probably. By now the sadness was long gone from his eyes, as well as any residue of other feeling it might have left behind. If there was anything there it was curiosity, as he watched me. He dipped the paint brush into a colour I'd never known him use for the mark before.

"No," he continued, "it was long after that that I knew... Claudette?" He said this, his voice entirely different from before, mocking, deliberately insincere, inviting me to disbelief of everything he had just said, inviting me to something else besides. He said it, and I suppose it is a mark of his talent that he was able to say it, and to look at my eyes, and at the same time to place on each of two side-by-side plates a tiny swirl of brown paint, a delicate circle flattened just enough to keep within the limits imposed by his mark. I knew his eyes were on me, but I couldn't take my own away from what he'd just done, the two tiny milk chocolate whorls, dead-centred and three-dimensional on the convex bottoms of the plates. When I looked up he was still watching me. I turned and walked away; but at the door I turned back. He was still watching me.

To this day I wish I'd been able to finish what I started to croak damply from the doorway.

"No way," I said, and stopped, hindered not by fear but by uncertainty that I would make myself understood.

My father continued watching, mistaking my meaning, I'm sure.

What I wanted to say, what I took with me through the door, and what I think after all my father might have understood, was:

No way, no damn way, are you ever making *me* Artistic.

But it didn't matter, the saying it, because he never did. Not in the way he had made, in descending order of speculation: Linda, Claudette, my mother. Not in the way he had made himself. Not, finally, in any way that mattered. No way. Fat chance.

*T*he Catch

"*It used to* be a bridge for the railroad," Pepper said, leading the way up the embankment. He was using his tour-guide voice. He got that from his father. "And then they changed it over for the highway." It was dark out, but when he turned to talk his blond hair shone from the moonlight, and his face was white as a ghost's, so I couldn't even see his freckles. I wondered if he was going to tell me again about the old railway tracks, how they tore them up to use as handrailings on the new bridges when the Overseas Highway connecting the Keys got built. The story was interesting and all when his father first told me. But since then I'd only heard it about a hundred times.

"And do you know what they did with all the old rails?" I just let him go on. The tail of the rope he was carrying dragged behind him. I could hear land crabs and other things, maybe rats, moving in the scrubby grass as we walked. The grunt grunted in the pail. He'd told me that too, about the grunt. When I'd caught it, fishing from the top of the bridge that afternoon, I'd thought it was a snapper. It looked a lot like a snapper.

We reached the fence at the top of the embankment. Pepper found the slit in the chain links and squeezed through sideways. He reached back through the slit and took the pail from me, holding it in the same hand as the rope. I squeezed

The Catch

through too. The grunt made more grunting noises. Maybe he knew what we were going to do to him.

We were on the bridge now, beneath the roadbed, on a sort of wide concrete ledge. It was a lot darker than before. Pepper took a few steps, feeling his way with one hand. I stayed still, and closed my eyes. I had a theory that closing my eyes would dilate my pupils faster. There was a sound of waves washing over the sand beaches on either side of the bridge. It was funny how you only ever noticed the sound at night. I concentrated on how funny that was for a while, trying to dilate. Then I opened my eyes.

Pepper was a few feet ahead, leaning over the ledge, looking down at the water. All around us were rusty girders and struts and beams running at different angles. Overhead was a wire mesh net, bulging with concrete chunks that had fallen away from the roadbed. Somebody had told me, Pepper's dad I think, that they were going to tear the bridge down soon. It was getting too dangerous. I looked at Pepper, standing on the crumbly concrete edge, and the way he seemed to be doing a balancing act, with the pail in one hand now and the coiled rope in the other. It seemed darker all of a sudden, even with the moon and stars and my dilated eyes. And quieter too, even with the chain and hook on the end of Pepper's rope scraping against a girder once in a while. And a little scary.

Then a truck went by overhead, flicking its high beams, and I was only afraid we'd get caught.

But then it was dead quiet again, and Pepper's hair was shining.

Pepper hopped onto a beam and took a few steps out over the water. I moved up to where he'd been standing and looked over the ledge. It was about twenty-five feet down. I could see green-glowing things a foot or so long skimming around just below the surface of the water. Otherwise the water was black, and no matter how hard I tried I couldn't see into it. I must have been holding my breath while I looked because I suddenly needed a big one, and it was funny, I could really smell the salt in the breeze, which ordinarily I didn't notice anymore. Then I looked at the black water again, and I knew that if a person fell in he'd never get out. After all, we were fishing for sharks.

"Fish," Pepper said, when he handed the pail back to me. I think he was talking about the green-glowing things. But he didn't use his tour-guide voice.

We both started walking along the beam, farther out over the water. Ahead, over Pepper's shoulder, I could see house lights still burning across the channel, on Big Pine Key. Through the girders, to the right, I could see the Gulf, and if I looked hard, off to the left on the ocean side, I could make out the little mangrove island, less than a quarter mile offshore. I always liked looking out across water, any water, and there was a cable running shoulder height alongside the beam that you could hold onto to keep your balance. I hung onto it. But Pepper kept his hands at his sides, walking fast.

It seemed we walked a long way. Every twenty feet or so the view was blocked by a pair of thick concrete pilings, running straight up to the roadway overhead and anchored deep below in the water, one on the Gulf side, one on the ocean. We passed between five or six pairs. We had to get far out, where the channel ran deep. That's what Pepper's dad had said. When we were about a quarter way out under the bridge we stopped.

Pepper seemed to know just what he was doing. I held the pail while he splashed around in it and finally got a hold of the grunt. Pepper held the fish flat on the beam. With the palm of his hand he pushed the tip of the big hook through its back, just behind its head. I could hear the crunch when the barb went through. The grunt still flipped around for a while and in the moonlight I could see the little pale blue stripes running from its snout up over the forehead and around its eyes. Pepper slashed the sides and slit the belly with his jackknife. "To make the shark think it's wounded," he said. I tied the free end of the rope to a girder like he told me and stood back. Then Pepper started whirling the hook and chain leader around in a circle by his side. I could feel little splashes on my face from the dead fish. I just tried to ignore it, screwing up my eyes so they wouldn't get wet and trying to focus at the same time on the dark channel, out where I figured the line would hit.

I guess Pepper's foot slipped or something. Because the next second I heard a splash right below us where the chain and hook must have hit the water. I watched the slack rope by our feet uncoil and kind of slither off the beam like a snake, real slow. And I was surprised when I looked up and found I was holding Pepper's shoulder so tight that the muscle in my arm hurt. Pepper was grinning hard as if he was going to be sick. Then he was just smiling, and I did too, forgetting for a moment to let go. After I did let go he said that he would have been okay, that he'd only lost his balance for a second. I looked down towards the water and at the few feet of line I could see before it disappeared into the dark. The line looked tight. The current must have been strong there. From the way Pepper hung onto the cable walking back, I knew it wasn't true, about him having been okay.

When we got back to our pup tent we rolled the flaps down over the front screen like we always did. Inside there weren't even stars to keep away the darkness and the first thing I always did was to feel around with my hands to make sure everything I couldn't see was still there. Nobody could see me anyway, and, after, it felt good to wriggle down and find my place in the sleeping bag.

When I did get settled I lay still. I could feel the heat from the day rising from the crushed coral, through the canvas floor, and into the sleeping bag. With my hand I could feel the spots on the bag where the cotton was stiff. And at the same time I knew that my parents were outside, in their silver Streamline trailer, with the light from the moon reflecting off it, and everything on the campsite tidy and clean and in order — immaculate is how my mother would put it, if she was really pleased with herself. I knew they'd be lying quietly together, my parents, breathing softly, sleeping.

I heard Pepper giggle next to me. He felt warm, like the sleeping bag, except I could feel him moving.

"Your hand's cold," he said, and he giggled again.

"Yours smells fishy," I told him, laughing because it was one of those times when just about everything seems funny. And then, "Tell me again about Joanne." Joanne was Pepper's next-door neighbour. He spied on her sometimes and one night especially, when she was in her backyard with her boyfriend. Her parents were away and she thought nobody was around. Joanne was fifteen and that night it was warm and she was wearing only a bikini. Other times when Pepper had told me I could see it just like it happened. I knew she looked a lot like my friend's older sister at home. I knew what she looked like naked. And I knew what her boyfriend did, how he felt, because I was there too. In my imagination. Pepper showed me.

But for some reason I couldn't concentrate that night, and it was strange in the dark the way I'd be thinking one thing and suddenly be thinking something else, then something else again. I thought of Dad, puking up his suppers more and more often the last couple of months. I thought of Pepper's dad, with his bald brown head and big belly and him having made a killing in real estate. I thought of Ralphy's older sister at home, not a bad guy even though she was a girl. I thought of the grunt, grunting, then hooked.

And all the time, kind of beneath this other thinking, I

The Catch

knew it was Pepper there whispering the story beside me, and that outside my parents were lying asleep in the trailer. Then I felt Pepper kind of jerk and I knew my hand didn't feel cold to him anymore. And soon his didn't smell fishy either, because there was another smell, the secret one. Our hands were slippery with it. We were blood brothers, like we decided before.

We got up early next morning. We'd been sharing the tent nearly a week, to keep each other company, but Pepper had to go home that day. Down the Keys aways, on Deer Key, that's where the Johnsons lived. That's why we were here, me and my parents, because Mr. Johnson lived nearby and Dad and he were best friends when they were young. And because Dad needed a rest from selling insurance. They went fishing every day in Mr. Johnson's boat, just the two of them, because they went way back together and they had a lot to talk about. I guess that's what they wanted me and Pepper to be, best friends. It sounded fun from all the stories about the old days Dad and Mr. Johnson told when Mr. Johnson stayed for supper and for beer afterwards. Dad especially told some funny ones. But then they'd get sidetracked and it would end up with Mr. Johnson talking about real estate deals and how Dad should have listened to him when he gave him the chance and how insurance wasn't the game it used to be. And that's when I could see Dad start to get tired again and his sunburn would start to bother him because he never could tan and I'd have to get the Solarcane for him. He never would use this kind of cactus leaf with smelly yellow sap in it that Mr. Johnson brought over. I heard Dad tell Mom there were limits to even Mr. Johnson's all-encompassing expertise and he'd be damned if he was spreading bloody weed jelly on his skin.

Anyway, it was almost the end of the vacation and Pepper

had to go home that afternoon. Since this was our last day together Pepper and I'd decided to swim out to the little island, the one I'd seen the night before from the bridge, on the ocean side. We'd never tried it before since it was so far out, but we figured we might find some good shells along the way, maybe some apple murexes or some tritons, or maybe even catch some lobsters. We were going early in the morning because it was low tide then and the water would be shallow enough we could even walk a lot of the way, if we wanted. We hurried and got our skin diving stuff together, our fins, masks and snorkels, and our catch bags. First, though, we had to pull in the shark line, just in case any boats came speeding under the bridge and didn't see it.

When Pepper found his gear he ran ahead over the crushed coral. Usually, especially in the morning, I had to go slower because the coral hurt my feet. They must have got tougher though, because I kept up alright. I felt pretty good.

The bridge was fun in the daytime. It was too early yet, but usually there were people fishing from the catwalk on top of the bridge. Once, somebody caught a lion fish and had to cut the line because of the poison barbs. And in the daytime you could walk out underneath the bridge and jump into the water, if you weren't afraid and watched for park rangers. I did it twice altogether, sinking deep, way down through cooler and cooler water, swimming up as hard as I could to get a breath. It was a little scary but it was worth it.

I think Pepper must have been feeling pretty good too by the time we got to the bridge. We climbed the embankment and dropped our diving stuff by the fence and were kind of wrestling to see who could get through the slit in the chain links first. I got through first and ran over to the beam. I hopped up and started running along it, out under the bridge, just holding my one hand lightly over the cable as I ran, looking straight ahead. Pepper followed, running too.

I was first to get to the rope. It wasn't so far out over the channel as it seemed the night before. Since we were both in a hurry to get into the water I started pulling hard on the rope as soon as I got my hands on it. And then I knew there was something wrong. Something heavy was on the line, but it was funny since it didn't pull back like a fish. Pepper must not have noticed because he told me to hurry up. Then he realized what was wrong and he helped me to pull.

The rope was fairly short, and soon we had it pulled tight, so it hung straight down to the water below us. We still couldn't see what was on it, but it was awful heavy. Together we counted to three and we heaved. And then we saw it, the mouth and the part of the shark's head that was up out of the water. The back half of the grunt was still on the hook dangling, just a few shreds of skin left where the head had been. We eased the rope back down again.

It seemed we stood there holding the rope for a long time. Finally I asked Pepper if he thought maybe it was still alive. Pepper didn't seem to hear me.

We let off some more slack and tied the rope off on a girder.

"It's damn big," Pepper said.

Not to be mean, but I pretty well knew that for myself. I asked him again if he thought it was alive.

"Na," he finally said. "It's dead. It's gotta be."

I thought it probably was too — dead, that is. But then again it might just have been tired. Pepper hadn't sounded all that sure either. We pulled the rope up to take another look. It looked dead.

For a few minutes we just stood there thinking about it. Then Pepper untied the rope and let out all the slack, holding the free end loose in one hand like he might want to let go fast. He started walking, hanging on tight to the cable with his other hand. From the way he began sort of hopping along after the first few steps, I could tell he was getting excited and probably wanted to get back to shore to show my dad what we'd caught. Neither Dad nor Mr. Johnson had caught anything near as big in all the time we'd been there. For some reason I felt kind of funny about showing my dad. I had a weird feeling in my stomach, probably because I hadn't eaten anything that morning. But it seemed to get worse when I thought of Dad seeing what Pepper and I had caught. It didn't seem fair. I thought we'd likely show him anyway. He'd be proud of us, and mad if he didn't get any pictures.

Soon Pepper couldn't walk any further with the rope. I'd seen it coming, but I hadn't said anything. The problem was the concrete pilings. Our beam ran between a pair of them and there was no way to pass the rope around the outside of either one. They were too thick. There were five more pairs between us and the shore.

Pepper didn't seem to know what to do. He had his mouth open part way, and I don't know why, that really started to bug me. But I just waited, twisting my head all around so I didn't have to look at him. Since he always wanted to do everything first, be the leader, I thought I'd let him figure this one out too. After a minute though, when Pepper had his back to me, I found I was staring at his tan, thinking how dark it looked with his blond hair that was really almost white. Then I looked down at my own legs and stomach and I was surprised to see I had as good a tan as he did. I'd always thought of myself as white, like I was at the beginning of the vacation. I felt terrific all of a sudden, just standing there behind Pepper's back, comparing tans. Which is petty, I knew. Mom would have said it was petty. Dad would have too. Maybe. Anyway, I didn't have the feeling in my stomach anymore. And I knew what to do about the shark. Pepper's mouth didn't even bother me anymore.

I took the rope out of Pepper's hands and tied it off. "I'll swim below," I said, "and you throw the rope down to me." He looked at me, like he couldn't quite understand. "You said it was dead." He was still being a little thick about things. But I have to admit I was a little scared myself. Not much though. I had it all planned out.

I ran back along the beam, over the crumbly concrete ledge that I hadn't even noticed much that morning, and through the slit in the fence, hitting it sideways with my shoulder, so it hardly slowed me up. I picked up my diving stuff and kept running down the embankment to the beach on the Gulf side of the bridge. I didn't stop until I was standing in the water, the little waves washing over my ankles.

The water was cold, and it was still too early for anyone else to be out, but those things didn't bother me. It was going to be a good morning. I could tell from the sky and the water, they were both so clear. I spit in my mask and rinsed it so it wouldn't fog and put it on. I slipped my fins on and put the mouthpiece of the snorkel in my mouth.

The cold water was a shock at first but I got used to it fast. I flutter-kicked out into the channel a ways, drifting with the current towards the bridge. Pretty soon the swimming started to seem like a game somehow. I kept my head down and concentrated on the sea bottom, even though I wanted to look up to see where I was. It was a contest to see if I could get to the right place without looking up from the water. It was hard too, because the sea bottom was so bare — none of the purple sea fans, no coral formations, not even any patches of sea grass — just sand, rippled like it is from the wind sometimes on the beach, as far as I could see. Even though we'd snorkelled nearby before I'd never noticed how bare the bottom was in the channel.

After a while, when I figured I was at exactly the right spot out in the channel and under the bridge, I lifted my head and looked up. I was right too. Overhead I could just barely see Pepper kneeling in the shadows underneath the bridge. When I raised my hand he threw the rope. It fell wide of me but I only needed a few kicks to get to it. Then I had it, the end wrapped tight around my hand, and I kicked hard and fast, with and across the current, towards the shore on the ocean side of the bridge. I was really moving, I guess it was my new fins — I'd only had them for a few days. I felt that if I just kicked hard enough I'd fly right up out of the water. Which is how it is sometimes when you get going like that with a current. Just flying.

That pace didn't last too long though. The rope pulled tight and all of a sudden I remembered what I was there for. I stopped swimming and treaded water for a minute, my back to the shore. I tried to follow the rope with my eyes, concentrating on where it blended in with the sand, but my snorkel flooded and a little water got into my mouth before I could blow the snorkel clear. It didn't bother me though. I was used to the taste. I tried again to see the end of the rope and what was on it, but I couldn't.

There didn't seem to be any other way so I started back-pedalling, hard but smoothly as I could, towards the shore, dragging the rope. That was the way you were supposed to handle a shark, I'd read it, by facing him and back-pedalling away, gently. Of course this one was dead and it was mainly because of the rope that I swam that way. But still, I was glad to be doing things the way you were supposed to.

It turned out to be a lot harder than I'd thought, swimming backwards against the current. But my legs were strong from so much skin diving before and finally I could see I was moving towards shore. My fins started kicking up sand after a while and I was in shallower water. Then I could walk.

When I got up on the beach there was still nobody around. I threw my mask and snorkel up on the sand and started hauling in the rope. And there he was, rolling in the shallow water. Rolling in a bit and rolling back out again in the little sandy waves. I could tell he was dead, because

The Catch

there's nothing else in the world that will roll around in the surf like that except something that's dead — dead fish, Portuguese men o'war, seagulls, they all seemed to roll that same way. And especially it wasn't natural for a shark if he had the least bit of life. I kneeled down to take a closer look.

There was a big hole in his lower jaw around the hook, a lot bigger than the hook. I guessed he'd really fought. I touched the skin. It was rough as sandpaper and grey, but a colour grey that made it hard to imagine he'd ever been alive. Already he'd begun to stink. A string of what looked to be his own insides was hanging from his asshole. I think it was an intestine. The smell got worse by the minute.

There was one thing I wanted to do, that you kind of have to do, just because it's a shark. I grabbed his snout and pulled it back to look at the teeth. It was what I expected. They were mean-looking and sharp. Some of them were broken from the hook. But he was dead. I looked at the round dead fish eyes. Dead.

Pepper was down from the bridge by then. He looked excited but he stood back. I think he didn't know whether to come and take a closer look, or run and get my dad. I think he was still a little afraid too.

"Sure does stink," he said. That much he knew from where he was standing. I didn't say anything, but I figured it was time.

I took the hook out, which was easy because of the big hole. I grabbed hold of the shark by the long part of the tail, the part that sticks straight up when he swims. I could get a good grip, not like a fish, because of the rough skin. I still had my fins on and they were splashing as I backed into the water pulling the shark behind me. I think Pepper said something but I didn't really hear. I wasn't paying much attention anyway. I backed into the water until it was up to my neck and then swam as best I could out a bit into the channel. I let

THE SAD EYE

him go. I didn't have my mask on, but even without it I could see him sinking, and then the grey shape of him lying on the sandy bottom. I swam back to Pepper on the shore.

Pepper and I swam out to the island that day. We didn't see any good shells. Just some conchs and tulip shells. And we didn't catch any lobsters, though Pepper went after a few. Their holes were too deep in the coral.

After supper Pepper's dad came to pick him up. My dad had been in the trailer most of the day, sick from the sun, he said. But he came out then and Mr. Johnson and him shook hands, holding on to each other's wrists with their free hands. They said stuff about doing it again next year and writing. Pepper and I shook hands too.

After the Johnsons left, I took down the pup tent and stored it away, so we wouldn't have to bother in the morning. Mom and I told Dad to stay in the shade and supervise and we got busy cleaning up and packing things.

That night I slept in clean white sheets on a bed in the trailer.

In the morning when it was still cool we hitched the trailer to the car and started the long drive up the Keys to the mainland. I had the back seat and it took a while for me to get settled into my usual spot on the passenger side where I could see the speedometer and the odometer when I wanted. There was this funny smell and I kept trying to find it. Then I decided it was probably from the car being shut up so much.

Mom wanted to play the same game we'd played on the way down. When we drove over a narrow key or a bridge she'd watch to the left and I'd look to the right to see who could spot the most interesting things in the water. On the way down I'd spotted a manta ray and two dolphins on the

The Catch

Gulf side of the Keys and Mom hadn't seen anything on the ocean side. I had the ocean side this time, she said.

Neither of us had much luck at first. But we weren't really trying. We were both waiting to get to the Seven Mile Bridge. It had a good view for a really long stretch.

I noticed the smell again, like medicine or crushed up weeds. A couple of times when we weren't going over any bridges I kind of checked around on the floor and on the bottoms of my sneakers and in the crack of the seat. And then we'd pass by water again and I'd be looking out there.

Finally we reached the Seven Mile Bridge. Since there was no construction work going on, Dad drove pretty fast. I took a quick look over to see how fast, and just then I saw Dad rubbing at the back of his neck. The smell got worse. And just for a second I saw the burned alligator skin on his neck was yellow. Cactus jelly yellow.

On the ocean side the water was really clear and I stared through the railings at it. But I didn't see anything in the water. And after a while the only things I noticed at all were the handrailings along the side of the bridge.

Something Is Coming

I could hear them. Almost as soon as I stepped out of the house, I could hear them. It was Sunday, morning, summertime, and very early, before even any of the Wilsons were up next door. Certainly before my parents were up. Early enough for the whole day to be in the air: dust, green, a faint rot from the Wilson place. Yes, I could hear them. They were coming — a high hum like would come from the tv early on a Sunday, when the target patterns were on, that's what it was like. A few early cars rolled along the main street, one over from ours; they'd disappear for long moments behind the houses which separated the streets, and each time, between held breaths, I wondered if they'd ever appear again, if they somehow didn't know. I checked quickly up and down our own street for signs of life. I tensed the muscles of my jaw and throat harder; somehow that tuned them in better. I was on the front line of our property now, beside the driveway, near the old maple. The hum became louder and higher pitched and I leaned against the tree, feeling weak. They were coming, from out of town, from the direction of the high school down the street and around the corner. Yes, definitely, I could hear them. But subterranean now. They had burrowed beneath the world and were digging out a whole complex under our town. I was the only one to hear, I had special hearing. They were right in my ears now, humming louder, coming, invading, carrying God knew what bombs

Something Is Coming

and machines, and I had to warn. But I was seven, I knew — an overweight, glasses-wearing seven and I knew that too — and who was going to believe? I thought of waking my parents but instead clenched harder and arched my back against the sound, upping the volume, willing the drums of my ears to burst against them, thinking, I think, to blow my whole self up against them. Next door some of the Wilsons were awake. I could hear one of them screaming — having the tar whaled out of him, I knew. In front of me the warm street began to melt, became tarry, undulated slowly. I leaned harder against the tree. And just before it ended, I was sure I saw a huge black whale-shaped object bobbing towards me, riding the earliest waves of heat on down the street.

* * *

When I was eight my father gave me his old RCAF cap, a few unravelling cloth badges, and a couple of stories from his Air Force days. The badges included a set of small white wings, strangely incomplete to me without an attached bird.

One of the stories was of how my father had tricked his mother, my grandmother, into letting him join the Air Force in the first place — the matter depended solely on her permission, he being only seventeen and his father dead. Apparently he had simply threatened to join the Navy, lying to her, saying how it had not the foolish age restrictions of the other branches of the service. As he well knew, my grandmother was terrified of water, having already lost one son to drowning. She consented.

Two things bothered me about the story. The first was that my grandmother should have been so unmotherly as to have missed a hole in the story my own mother would have detected on her most distracted days: my father too was terrified of water, doubtless for the same reason, and would never have volunteered for the Navy. (Something that didn't bother me: the detail of my young uncle drowning at a public beach while my father, helpless non-swimmer, watched. I accepted it as simply that — a detail, a good memory-sticking one, but only slightly more important than the non-detail of my dead grandfather, who was simply absent from the story, a non-character.) The second thing was a matter of both joy and confusion. In all other cases I had known, the chiefest sin in the world was to lie to one's parents, especially one's mother. But my father seemed proud of his deception. Somehow he communicated the "official line" to me, that, what with friends and relatives turning up in the papers dead or missing almost every month, signing up by any means possible was naturally the patriotic and manly thing to do. I tried to believe it: I liked the story. I checked my own situation for possible parallels. This was a tale I could relate to, a story told son to son. And it was as a son that I finally knew my father's real joy and the truth of the thing: he had put one over on a parent and got away with it.

But, try as I might to see them, there were no wars for me, at eight. No handy populations of the dead to set me free from the rigours of truthtelling.

The other war story I still remember was of my father's boxing career. At seventeen and for a couple of years after, until the war ended and he was discharged, my father had been a fighter. He had met in the ring, he said, many men older and bigger than he and often come out the victor, though he stressed that this last part was unimportant. He told of one particular bout in which he had fought an especially large man, a Pole. It was a grudge match, he said, explaining this simply meant the rules were relaxed a little. He told of being smashed and smashed almost from the beginning, of feeling punch drunk, deaf to the bells, insensible to everything near the end but the smack of fists against his stomach and the smell of salt and leather from his own gloves weakly held in front of his face. He didn't remember the final blow that put him out, but he told of how he wanted to keep on going after the smelling salts brought him around. All the while he told it, his fists were clenched and dancing over his big present-day belly, swollen from years of selling on the road, but still hard for all its size. It was an effective device, these father's fists; I took the story deep into my own gut. This one, I knew, was somehow different. My relationship with the hero had changed; I didn't know which of the characters I identified with. I didn't even know which my father identified with, his fists so ambiguously bobbing: the Pole smashing, or his young self being smashed. And, deep down, I must have wondered which he identified me with, for it must have been clear at some level that this story, at least this story, worked that way too. He never offered to teach me to box and I never asked to learn, even after the couple of times I came home with torn clothes and a blackened eye. Afterwards, though I knew it wasn't so, as he had told it, I thought of my father's drowned brother, somehow in this story too.

That was the presentation made to me at eight, a single event, however much the necessary moods for the different givings and tellings seem now to me impossibly disparate to be of a piece. The badges, I remember, were squirrelled away to whatever secret place in my room I was using at the time for such valuables — I think to the vacant space beneath the bottom drawer of my dresser. The stories were stored wherever stories are stored (somewhat less carefully than the badges, I think; for despite my immediate visceral involvement, I was finally a little disappointed: when my father was discharged at nineteen, he almost immediately took the first step on the road to becoming a salesman and family man, never having left Canada, never having experienced any of the action I think we both wanted for him).

The hat was the only thing that stayed out. It went to the collection of hats I had somehow built up and drew on for my occasional dress-up sessions. Unforgettable these, primarily because they have become a part of my mother's family mythology, become public, to be hauled out and told over when old friends and relatives gather. They were very private at the time, performed solely for my mother at quiet times after school or on Saturday afternoons when my father was on the road. They consisted almost entirely of the simple donning of a hat — sombrero, sailor's, mountaineer's, beret and, now, air force — and assuming what I considered the appropriate posture of whatever character I was trying to be. There were never words to these performances. The story existed purely in the hat, and in my mind, and in my mother's laughs and praise. It was not until some months after my father gave me his old air force hat that I connected it with flying. It was as my mother prepared supper, one weekday, that I finally took off, soaring higher and higher around the kitchen on the currents of her laughter.

There is one other thing that I used to do at this age, which somehow seems important.

Next door to us was an old house. It looked old anyway, since barely a chip of paint remained on the wooden slats which sided it, many of which had lost their nail holds and hung at more or less right angles to the rest. But for one corner which sagged, it was a perfectly rectangular house, flat-roofed, two-storied. The Wilsons — consisting of varying numbers of adults and babies, and a whole slew of boys, maybe six, all of them older than I — lived there. I think the children were all consigned to the top floor, since it was here where the screen windows were most tattered, at those windows that had any; sometimes, looking out my own bedroom window at night or even during the day, a glistening arc of pee could be seen issuing from one or another of them. It is funny, I must be remembering the house only as it was during the summer, for certainly there must have been storm windows up in the winter.

During those summers, the two or three clustered around my eighth year, I often used to spend large amounts of time indoors, in my room, reading comic books, children's mysteries, chapters from old Books-of-the-Month, anything. The few friends I had from school all seemed to live on the other side of town, or farther, in the near countryside, too far to go see most days.

Occasionally, I would help my mother with her rock garden in the backyard, watch really, her hands tough as weed stalks among the marigolds, pansies, geraniums — always common flowers, like the cheap straw beach hat she wore for the work, or the tunes from television commercials she would hum. But the plot was small, like a little quarter pie abutting the Wilson yard and that of the old spinster woman who lived behind us, never needed much attention, so it was seldom I was in the yard for this purpose. It was seldom I spent other time with my mother either, for she was somehow less interesting inside the house, and seemed always busy.

Often though, in my room reading, I would hear the voices of the Wilsons next door, the slap of a ball in leather mitts as they warmed up for a baseball game. At first I must have just watched from my window; but eventually I ended up perched — shyly at first, then boldly — on what became my seasons' seat for the games, the top of the wooden picnic table in our backyard. It was here where I spent much of my outdoor time during these summers, watching the group of older boys (at any time at least two or three must have been Wilsons) play baseball.

It was a small yard where they played, bordered off from ours precisely as any fence by the line where our neatly clipped lawn ended and their knee-high weeds began — with the small exceptions of our rock garden, which oozed over slightly onto their property, and a few rotting stumps on the lot line, sawed off cleanly at ground level. Because of the yard's size, I think the boys must have intentionally checked their bat swings, although flys sometimes would arc through the air over the high hedge at the back of their property. More often it was line drives and pop flys they would hit, and, good spectator that I became, I would keep my eye always on the ball, growing dizzy as a player struggled through the tall grass, his mitt open to the sky for a fly, or cringing, my eyes half closed, as a drive punched into a glove held only inches from someone's face. Finally though, it was the less spectacular grounders which accounted for the most home runs, for then the ball invariably became lost in the grass for vital seconds while the runner took his bases and the two or three players of the opposing team frantically kicked through the grass. Sometimes it took the combined efforts of both teams to finally locate a ball, and in about one in every three games they never would find it and would either come up with another or end the game.

From my patient, spectator's outpost at the picnic table, though, I could pretty well have told them at any given time where a dead ball lay. I never did, because, I suppose, I had never said anything to the Wilsons before, or they to me. But it wasn't really that, and it wasn't a matter of shyness or even childish reserve. I felt passionately involved in the game, with the Wilson gang, and they seemed to accept my involvement. They never invited me to play, but they never jeered or teased me, as I realize now they might have. It was as though it was all part of the rules. And it didn't matter that the object for me — that the ball eventually be lost — was somewhat different from theirs. After it was lost I had my own game plan to follow: never for a moment taking my eyes away from a dead ball; patiently waiting for the game to be played out or to stop if they found no alternative ball; more waiting for the appropriate amount of time to pass after they did leave; crossing the property line; swishing through the grass directly to the spot; and the glorious confirmation of power as I bent and held in my hand the thing that had eluded all the others. After that, I would take my prize home and put it in the carport. If they played again the next day, and if I watched, I would sometimes toss the ball over to them, without a word. Sometimes I didn't. I don't know why the inconsistency. Over the weeks, the summers, I collected a number of balls — softballs, hardballs, sponge balls, tennis balls; in all kinds of conditions — new, so that there was barely a scuff mark or a grass stain on them, or so old that there would be hunks torn out or horsehide covers flapping or completely gone. The quality had nothing to do with whether they were returned or not. Maybe that is why the Wilsons never suspected me. At least, I think they never suspected me.

I never knew personally the Wilsons, any of them, although a couple were only a year or two older than I. Later on, as I progressed in grade school, I knew *of* them, for there were always stories of a Wilson involved in whatever minor crime had happened in town — joyriding in stolen cars, underage drinking, that sort of thing. Also, the whole family seemed to be athletic, and the two things together made them famous among their peers. We nodded amiably, I eagerly, when we passed in the street, since we were, after all, neighbours. In high school, I even attended the same parties with some, although always we were in slightly different circles, which would sometimes rub or even mesh edges, but never merge. There were always those barriers of fame and age and something else, as though we were embarked on paths which were parallel, but *only* parallel, and it wasn't a matter of simply catching up.

This was the way I knew them later. At eight I knew them, other than through my own observations, through one story, and this very much like the war stories my father told, retrieved from, stored in, the same place.

I remember it as a kind of parable, although the moral, the end of it, became changed over the years. Ricky Wilson (that has always been his name, Ricky, to my family, to me, despite his final middle age, despite the seemingly incontrovertible "Richard" in newstype), Ricky Wilson, then, has always been something of a legendary character to me. Never, I think now, was he one of the ballplayers next door. I never saw him once, or never distinguished him if I did. I think by then he already was married, already was having a hard time of it too. The story of the Wilsons I heard when I was eight or so, and then again later, was of Ricky and a time when he was perhaps twelve or thirteen — before my time, or just about when it was beginning. It must have been just after my parents moved into the house I have always known as ours, a couple of years after my father began his career as a salesman. It is a story which came from my mother.

It helps to recall that we lived near the high school in town — about three blocks from it, but not on any pathway to or from anything of importance to several generations of teenagers. This left the school of little threat to our property while still conveniently close when I attended. It was convenient, too, for the Wilsons, those who attended for any length of time. It was convenient for Ricky, in 1955 or so, though he was of course too young to attend.

At that time the high school still had a militia. It is hard for me to imagine what was done there — much marching and drilling and exercising no doubt; perhaps it was credit in some way towards a diploma. I would be surprised if any of the young cadets had to resort to my father's elaborate trickery to gain permission to join. In any case, there were guns there — that irresistible lure to young men, compensation for so much that is boring. And Ricky Wilson knew of them. At twelve, knew enough, too, to be able to outwit the Canadian Militia. At least for a time. He and one of his brothers (he was never identified in the story) broke into the school one Sunday during the summer holidays. When the police finally found them they were in the top storey next door, trying to load two submachine guns with the wrong ammunition. I suppose they were justly punished. I don't remember precisely how my mother put it, but that must have been the moral of the story, at first.

For me at eight the story was a good one, a vivid one. I could imagine a Wilson or two up in the top storey of the house next door, the screens flapping in the warm summer breeze, the quietness of Sundays on our street; their fear-tinged excitement and then the frustration of trying to jam the wrong bullets into the magazine. I could easily flip sides and imagine the police knocking on the loose screen door of the Wilson's box-like house, tramping up the squeaky stairs, uncertainly smoothing down their own guns at their sides as they tried to anticipate two children, their own townspeople, with machine guns; the sweat prickling the close cut hair of their necks. I could look up from my bedroom window and imagine this as easily as I could a silvery ribbon of pee showering down, as yet another Wilson pissed upon the world.

This is the story, and the first moral which I believe my mother meant to go along with it — that of bad children being punished for wrongdoing. I think she was never quite comfortable with it. When I was older I thought she had initially liked the tale because Ricky had stolen something impractical, not like money, but that also the possibility of our own neat home, my mother's little garden vulnerable as a child, coming under seige from above had bothered her. I thought she would have preferred they steal something else, an outhouse, or no, one of the miniature plaster livery boys which proliferated on the lawns of the town as it prospered over the years.

At twelve I heard the same story again. My mother liked to get the most possible educational mileage from her stories. And though she would never tamper with the facts of a real life fable, she was a good-hearted woman; she liked a happy ending. The version of the story I heard at twelve had a slightly different ending, or rather beginning, from the first one.

By that time Ricky had been married for several years, although for the first of them he had been something less than a model husband and father, and far less than a model employee at several different jobs. Somehow (I didn't know how, for my parents seemed to have even less contact with the Wilsons than I) word had gotten around that Ricky had straightened out his life. He had been working steadily at the auto assembly plant in the nearby city, his wife was happy, and his two children were looking healthier and cleaner for it. That was how she put it, beginning with this latest information, and harkening back. Ricky's past, the incident with the guns (the town's militia no longer existed, a fact she was quick to point out), was at once an amusing example of an only slightly excessive precocity and a benchmark in the measure of his final rise to success in the adult world. With steadiness, she suggested, I too would someday rise.

Something else happened around my twelfth year, shortly after the second telling of the Ricky story. It is a scene which has always stayed with me. One of my own stories. It occurred on one of our family outings to the city for the shopping, usually clothes, which we didn't do in town. This was in the summer of 1967, and the city we lived closest to was Windsor, Ontario.

Far more vivid than any of the newspaper photographs or televised news footage of flaming buildings or dark masses of people scattering or milling or looting were the clouds of smoke hanging low over the Detroit skyline as we drove down Ouellette Avenue towards the downtown department store my mother preferred. In the front seat one of my parents, I don't remember which, said in a low voice *It's the riots* and the words, the breath of them, hung there in our overheated car, as dark and quiet as the smoke we were watching. It was as though the mere news of the event hadn't made it real to them either, and, looking out across the river to the States, I suddenly knew what they did: that people *were* burning buildings, smashing windows — buildings and windows not very different from those in our town. And I could *almost* know in the same way that people were being shot and were shooting back. As my father looked for a place to park, there was further low talk in the front seat of how the borders had been closed off. I craned my head a little out the window to see better, until my mother told me to get back in. But the scene, the extraordinariness of it, seemed to allow for disobedience, seemed to allow for so much more, and it wasn't long before I had let go of the knowledge that had almost come home to me and was hanging half-way out into the confusion of traffic. Something else, some important thing, I felt, was going to end with the stopping of the car, and my mind raced. How long, I wondered, before the flames backed the fighting hordes up against the far shore? before they started swimming across? or expropriated the docked freighters for the short trip? I knew vaguely of a navy yard somewhere in Michigan and I armed the crowds with choice pieces of weaponry recalled from old war movies: with submarines, torpedoes, and aircraft carriers brimming with Kamikaze planes. And the whole thing wasn't frightening now, as it almost had been; in the slowly moving car, in the car now stopping, I wanted to be right down at the river watching. And I wanted to be *there* too, on the other side of the river, among the excitement, protesting, demonstrating, rioting, I wasn't sure which, half a dozen news stories had all blended together; thought it merely a matter of being allowed to observe just a little longer. Thought it simple as making a long standing broadjump, *à la* Superman, from one side of the river to the other, once things became clear.

But then we parked, and with the warm sidewalk beneath my feet as real as the river and what was beyond, I allowed myself to be shepherded into the store.

Later, at home again, I decide that something had happened on the car trip. For me, "across the river" had always referred to the whole of the United States, and had often been the vague setting of all my vague longings. Now I knew for sure. I could see enough to know that the violent Detroit of 1967 was not quite what I wanted. But Freedom, that's what was going on over there. In the States, or at least in the cities — that's where it was. In California, perhaps, or in Washington, D.C., or even in Vancouver. Just barely out of my grasp, just a few miles beyond the river. Just a few years in the future.

So I prepared myself — such a bodily process it was too at that age, tensely counting over the faces and bodies of girl classmates in bed at night, struggling increasingly long and hard each time I came due to have my hair cut. On the intellectual front, I became opposed to the Vietnam war, though it was some time before I had any notion of why I ought to be or dared mention it to anyone. I would have read revolutionary texts, but there was none at our school library that I could discover. I had to make do with the juicier passages in adult spy novels and in one particular work of fiction I kept hidden in our meagre grade school stacks, ordered (by mistake no doubt) by the aging Miss Pear, our librarian. Though I forget the title, I still remember the plot of it: purportedly science fiction, it involved the take-over of the world by a phenomenally fertile tribe of migrating Eskimos, who bred ever faster and frantically as they approached more ideal conditions; who, throughout the whole course of the novel, were headed south.

By the time I was fourteen I had begun going to the high school near our home. My struggle against having my hair cut had netted me little more than a fluffy duck's tail by then, a half inch or so of hair carefully lapped over the rims of my ears, and longish bangs which were not fashionable even in my unkempt circles, but which I kept since it was after all hair and it helped to camouflage some of my newly acquired acne spots. The rest of these were inexpertly caked over with a hideously coloured cream then, and perhaps still, famous among adolescents. My reading material and bedtime enumeration of female classmates had not changed at all.

Living so close to the school I soon found out had both advantages and disadvantages. Since I was a townie, I had no cause to ride the big orange-coloured buses, the raucous conduits connecting the countryside for miles around with our grimy-bricked centre of learning. I always felt I missed out on something because of this, some special intimacy or secret fun which the others, those who gathered in groups at the end of the day, were privy to. But still, I heard enough complaining of early morning risings to realize, almost from the beginning, that I wouldn't like to trade places for long.

With the school so close, I was able to sleep in relatively late in the mornings. I would arrive at eight-thirty, in time for a visit and a carefully cuffed cigarette with my bussed-in classmates behind the school before the eight-forty-five bell sucked us as a group, flicking butts, towards our homerooms, like so much smoke ourselves. It is hard to recall what we talked about together then. Everything and nothing, I suppose. About girls, about various school sporting events. I remember our teasing each other about new hair cuts, while at the same time dreading the impending ordeal ourselves.

Remember our coarse, ill-informed joking about sex, never fully a joke, always tinged by nervousness. These two were recurring subjects, haircuts and sex, both never talked of seriously, both of the utmost seriousness to us. And recalling harder, it seems as though all our joking, perhaps all our social lives, was informed by the vibrating tautness of our highly secret lives, by some high-pitched, just-below-the-surface hysteria.

Remembering it like this, the whole thing returns in the form of the most primary impressions. Smells: sweat and acne lotion and damp clothes; semen and cigarette smoke and the vague sewer odour of the waste treatment unit fenced in at the back of the school lot where the buses collected, the newest thing at our school when I attended. And sounds: the scuffle of hundreds of teenage feet, the thud and abrupt exhalations of breath as footballs or basketballs or soccer balls, depending on the season, connected with bodies, the whine of the water pump of the waste unit out back, after it clicked on according to some mysterious timing of its own. And other sounds somehow like this: the buzz of the hallways or the morning groups outside, during the few moments before I would become a part of it myself; the sound of the television, after the stations had gone off the air for the night. Like what I had heard at seven years of age, when perhaps my hearing had been affected by high blood pressure caused by excess weight. I was no longer overweight, having shot up a good three inches at puberty, and having discovered the swimming pools in the city where I took lessons twice a week. And here was another of these sounds: the sustained ringing in my ears when I would swim lengths underwater during the free minutes at the end of my lessons; the increased intensity of the ringing after I had touched the far end of the pool and had doubled back beneath the surface to try for a second length, lungs threatening to suck themselves inside out, struggling between the need to surface, to drag in air, and to do a few last frantic breast strokes which were never enough to bring me back to my starting point. Perhaps most closely, this was the same sound the pump would make when it clicked on during those fifteen minutes in the morning. Always I would be distracted when that happened. Sometimes, but for the call of the school bells and the forward drag of my moving fellow smokers, I felt I would like to have stayed behind for a moment with the sound of the pump. The lure of that hum in all its different forms, the smells, the tensions of various muscles, these were my life to puberty.

By the time I was sixteen my hair was progressing: my ducktail had fanned out so that it now almost brushed the bottom of my collar; the hair over my forehead was now so long that I could nibble on it in idle moments and had to brush it aside to see. I still used this front hair to conceal spots on my forehead, but no matter how arranged, it could not disguise a rebellious new group appearing and reappearing on my chin with the regularity of flashing neon lights.

And so at home, my father's belly was progressing, becoming larger and less firm, and he seemed to be growing more tired. That winter, he gave me his old Air Force tunic, reiterating some of his old war stories, and imagining, it seems to me now, a version of his seventeen-year-old self in my unlikely lanky form. This could not have lasted for long, the illusion. The slouch of my shoulders did not conform at all to the boxed ones of the jacket, which was fine with me; I saw the uniform as a variation of the Army jackets popular with my set at that time. I had seen such fashions, remnants from war, a protest against it, on the rebels in televised demonstrations and on some of the other boys at school. In fact, in addition to these, there was a whole separate group at school who wore similar jackets, with jeans and ratty T-shirts, as I did, which I did not count. Their hair was perpetually short — not finally-caught-by-the-barber short, but militarily short. These were the few who owned their own jackets, had not picked them out of attics or found them in Salvation Army stores. These were the ones who spent their summers in the Militia, granted making some money and even travelling, but at the awful price of such shorn hair. I don't know what the jackets meant to them, Wednesday night voyagers to the city armory, some sixteen miles away. Probably no more than mine to me with my own Wednesday nights in the city, breath-holding and trying for that second length underwater. All I knew then was that I would never choose to have my hair cut to such ridiculous lengths for mere money, an attractive jacket.

By this time I had graduated to the tenth grade, and my group in the mornings behind the school had become more defined. There were three besides me, members of a couple of different buses who were my friends, who would gather with me during the mornings, accepting others on the periphery at different times, but always a solid unit, more or less loyal to each other. There was Tim, the smallest and fastest and cheapest of us, always hoarding cigarettes to himself, always way ahead of us on the track during gym class. There was Phil, whose father was a cattle breeder, quite literally, for he used to carry around in his car a huge stainless steel tank filled with liquid nitrogen and frozen samples of semen; Phil was often teased about this, was the quietest one perhaps because of it, and was my best friend at the time. And there was Evan, a city boy up until high school, privy to the mysteries of the city — to firsthand knowledge of girls and local sports figures and, through friends he still maintained, to the glamorous high school drug world which the rest of us knew only through television.

By now, together, we were more confident than we were

the year before, no longer the youngest, in the *tenth* grade. Others, the twelves and thirteens, were still far away from us, almost as far as adults, though not quite: the huge-muscled hockey and football players, the student councilmen, those over-life-sized sexual beings, the senior girls. But we did alright. We knew the school, had our own groups; and although we were still ineffective with girls, the most intriguing of those from our own grade having been already taken up by older men, there were still a few loyal to their peers and, of course, the latest batch of ninth graders to appraise from afar.

Also, near the end of that year, briefly, there was for me the school paper. I don't know how I got onto that, a mistake really, something I agreed to do during a moment of school spirit kindled by a crowd I did not usually hang out with. Somebody from my English class asked me to join.

I began to attend the weekly layout sessions. I met the senior girls who became slightly more human-sized, but no less sexual. In bed at night, I thought long hot thoughts about them; going to sleep, their images would mingle with thoughts of stories, with editorials on the poor quality of the cafeteria food, with elegiac news of our sad, cellar basketball team, with our groan-funny advice column. I began to read newspapers, and soon I was scalping, if not stories, at least ideas, style, from the legitimate news. I forget what was actually going on in the news at that time; I suppose if I stretched myself I could remember. But mostly what I am left with now is the feeling of it. There were things going on out *there* that were not happening *here*. The things *there* were of course bigger, but not too big, far, but not too far, like the senior girls. I tried writing about it a couple of times for the paper, the there and the here, but it seemed foolish when I set it down, and not at all what my editor was after.

There is only one news event from around this time that does stand out in my mind, and that is because I was involved with it. It is an event I never wrote about. By that time I had quit the newspaper in a fiery burst of principle over some small matter I can no longer recall.

It was after a long summer of odd jobs and hitch-hiking to indeterminate destinations around the county with Tim and Phil and Evan. It was in the fall of our eleventh grade year. I was still reading newspapers then, despite having quit the school paper. I should say I was still reading as I always had, not absorbing much, not so much for news as for fodder to feed my own aggrieved sense that something was happening and I was not involved, that huge injustices were taking place, the biggest being that I was still too small, would never have time to grow large enough to rectify the rest. Things were still happening too fast, were still too far away. Everything was over before I had even read about it, let alone grown old and able enough to act.

But I did read about the proposed nuclear testing in Amchitka. It took several weeks of reading the same information repeated, inured skimmer I had become, before it dawned on me that this event was in an important way different from the rest. And then it did, and it was as though the various related stories had taken on a single voice, calling me home after school, a little louder each day for a week or so, to listen to it. There were things happening, it said. Big things. There were movements afoot. All over. Across the country in Vancouver. In the United States, in California and Washington and Michigan. In France. Around the world. We were to raise up our voices again, the young and concerned of the world. It was to be like the sixties. *We* would say and *they* would listen, because there were so many of us. And best of all, the *it* was a possibility: there was to be a meeting of countries on the bridge between Windsor and Detroit, bare miles from our town. We, two groups, would each walk halfway across, join forces, against all authority.

And it hadn't happened yet.

I talked with Tim and Phil and Evan about it. They were enthusiastic from the first, surprising me, making me feel closer to them than I ever had before. The demonstration was to be held on a school day. So much the better, so much more perfect. We would be truant, but we would have a cause, be in the right, martyrs whatever the punishment, we decided in our heavily ironic way; truly Young Idealists, Romantics, Utopians, and two or three things besides. Then we discussed our reasons for going as seriously and as best we could so we might have at least some justifying ammunition when our parents found out, after the excitement. We decided to meet on the morning of the event, as usual behind the school, and then to hitchhike in.

The day of the protest we did meet, in our usual group among the unloading buses. We talked together of the plan, in low voices, conspiratorially. The others seemed to sense something was up, our air of exclusiveness, for a couple of the boys who sometimes stood with us did not come over, and one walking towards us actually veered off to another group before he arrived. We lowered our voices even more.

We continued talking, waiting for the final buses to pull away. Then they did. And in a few minutes the bell sounded and the rest of the students walked towards the back doors of the school, a few glancing over their shoulders at us. We tried genuinely to act casual now. We pretended to be deep in conversation, as though pausing for just a few final words, a few last drags of cigarettes before moving on. It was hard to feel inconspicuous. But the last of the others did vanish through the doors, our conversation abruptly stopped and for a few moments there was a complete silence, a short limbo. Then the sewage treatment unit clicked on, humming.

It startled me. For the very first time, I realized, I had stayed behind the bell; could stay for as long as I wanted, listening to the hum and the silence. But I didn't. The others somehow took the click as a signal — I too I suppose — and we ran as a group, stopping again around a shielding corner, Tim and Evan straggling on ahead before they realized that Phil and I had stopped.

We decided to hitch in pairs and to meet at the bridge. Tim claimed to know the way, so he went with Phil, the two of them breaking into a run again, heading up the road that ran behind the school and intersected the highway out of town. Evan and I tried to dawdle behind, but with the others running before us we were unable to keep still, skipped back and forth across the sidewalk, twirled in circles, unable to contain ourselves: only now did it seem we had truly crossed the line, were putting it over on someone, everyone, and were getting away with it. Up ahead the traffic seemed to have sensed the importance of our mission, of us: we watched a car stop for Phil and Tim almost as soon as they put their thumbs out. We jogged the rest of the way up to the highway and across it to take our place on the shoulder. I realized then how we'd been keeping our voices low, despite our excitement and our distance from the school, as though we were afraid of being overheard. Finally out on the road, it seemed we had made another step. I felt I should yell something, but I could think of nothing. Then the thing to do occurred to me. Loudly clearing my throat and with extravagant gestures, I began enumerating my clothes for Evan. *Demonstration Shoes*, I said forcefully, with a sweeping of my hand and in the voice of a salesman demonstrating shoes; these were calf-high boots, not that anyone could tell beneath the ample denim swishing from my knees to the ground. *Protest Pants*: jeans very wide-legged, faded, and as tight in the ass as a hot water wash and extra spin-dry the night before could make them. *Radical T-Shirt*: maroon and also very tight, seldom worn since I didn't feel my physique quite ideal for such fits; but I wore my jacket too. And finally, here, with these clothes, on such a mission, my jacket was perfect, my slouching shoulders appropriate: *Rebel Jacket*. Evan laughed. A car passed by us, then another, and I flipped defiant hair from my eyes, made confident, rude gestures at the dull olden faces inside. After ten or fifteen minutes, Evan and I began tossing bits of gravel at each other, tousled to keep warm. Another fifteen and we grew cold and bored and our enthusiasm flagged. We would have considered returning to school but for the certainty that the others were waiting on ahead for us, warmer, on top of the action, having some sort of fun we were missing. But for the fact that classes had already started for the day without us.

Two and a half hours later we did reach the bridge, thanks to Evan's navigation and several short rides. The last was from a farmer in a truck, headed to the city to pick up a part for his wife's car. He was an old man who chatted about his wife, the weather; he didn't ask us what we were doing out of school, didn't comment on our hair or clothes. He went out of his way to let us out at the right spot.

When he did let us out we found we were right on the edge of a crowd — not a very big crowd, less than that for a football game at our high school. But this was it, no doubt about it; we could tell from the signs leaning against the legs of some of the people. We looked immediately around for Phil and Tim, but couldn't see them. The crowd seemed to be focused on a toll booth up ahead; but I couldn't see the bridge, the one thing I had pictured clearly in my mind, and gazing around almost in a circle, disoriented, I couldn't even see the river. Still there was no sign of Phil and Tim. Behind us I noticed the farmer's pick-up truck slowly edging into traffic.

THE SAD EYE

Evan and I decided to go into the crowd to see if we could find the others, and we started edging our way through. As we got nearer to the toll booths we could see the police, helmeted, large in their uniforms, cordoning off the roadway. They were carrying small clubs — weighted with lead, heavier and more effective than baseball bats, I'd read. We overheard someone say they had completely closed down the bridge. I was still trying to see the bridge, the water. I still wasn't even quite sure which direction they were in: the pavement of the entrance came curving in off the street where the old man had let us off, curved past customs buildings, could have kept on curving right back in a circle for all I could see. I tried to overhear more from the group next to us, but they seemed to have closed themselves off. There were low acrid clouds of marijuana smoke hanging over their heads and those of some of the other groups, and Evan with a nod of his head pointed out the joints being passed around in cupped hands. Evan pulled out his Export A's and we smoked too, cuffing the cigarettes from habit.

We waited another fifteen minutes, though for what I don't know: the police didn't seem likely to move. By then Evan was making a great show of looking around for Phil and Tim, occasionally saying he thought he recognized someone he knew from the time when he used to live in the city. It never turned out to be the right person, but he seemed to be physically moving away from me, ready to rush off at any time towards an old friend. I looked too, at the people Evan pointed out, at ourselves, at the people around us. There were university students there; I could tell some of these, they looked like they were supposed to: something like us, only older. But looking around at the different small stands of people, there was another type too, older-seeming than the rest, but maybe not. Just different. They seemed dirtier somehow — not dirty like Evan and I were from hitching by the roadside, but dirty like they'd been that way a long time, like they weren't going to stop being like that when they got home that night. Some had ragged-looking clothes on, but not like us with our frayed pant cuffs, me with my nearly thirty-year-old jacket. There were few women or girls in the crowd. Some of the men had beards, some just hadn't shaved for a few days, and some simply looked like they hadn't; I touched the sparse hairs alongside my ears where I was trying to grow sideburns. It was different. These were the wrong people. We were the wrong people. Like we were already from different countries. Evan knew it, I think, and now I knew it too. With everyone in little groups, talking, it seemed, only among themselves, it was as though we were all lined up for something, a movie — one that Evan and I were too young to be admitted to, if anyone cared to notice, which they didn't. I overheard from another group some talk of rushing the police barricade and for a moment I tried to make myself believe it would really happen, grabbed Evan's arm, and tried somehow to project the feeling of it onto the crowd. But no. We weren't the group for it, weren't a violent group. Weren't really a group at all. We were all individuals, waiting docilely for the movie to begin.

Evan and I kept our look-out for Phil and Tim for a little while longer, the two of us acting, by then, as if that were the only reason we'd come, to meet friends. When we finally did walk away, Evan gave a disgusted glance back over his shoulder, his impression of what a person stood up looked like. I looked too. And away from the crowd, I could see what the movie was we'd come to see. The group, waiting, in their ragged clothes and dirty beards — they looked like old black and white film clips I'd seen of the Depression days.

We spent the rest of the afternoon until it was time to go home at the McDonald's, drinking coffee, eating small hamburgers, splitting orders of fries, and grumpily wondering what had happened to Phil and Tim.

* * *

If this were another kind of story it would end here. It would be about some kind of death or revelation, the ceasing of that buzz that called to me in so many different pitches and guises. It would be about the crossing of some line, the seeming lack of importance of the crossing, and the necessity of it all the same.

Perhaps some day I will make it end here, and the feeling that occasionally came back in later years in the form of a couple of different loves, several grand ambitions, will be a different one, another story. Perhaps; though even now, at rare times, walking a quiet street, something similar will come over me, a feeling that is almost physical, almost audible, going on inside, preparing me, arming me. I'll check down the street for I don't know what, half expect people to burst out from nearby houses needing me, requiring some out-of-the-ordinary action of me; requiring that I break through something precious and inhibiting, like love or fear.

Something happened at the bridge, or at least should have happened there. It violates the sense of story instilled in me by my parents, my nature, that I can't lay my finger on it, or even imagine something suitable.

One day, maybe, my father will have died on that day. He didn't. It was not until several days after then, my short absence from school miraculously still undetected by all, that he even suffered the first of the heart attacks that eventually finished him. And that first was a very minor one, taking him out for only eight or nine days. It was not until a year later, riding hard still his round salesman's belly and hoping for early retirement, that he succumbed to a larger one.

But for now it seems impossible, even callous, to use my

father in this way. He is part of a larger story, one which perhaps includes this.

All I can think to do is include the essence of a story that came in over the wire a few years ago at the small Alberta newspaper where I worked then: Richard Wilson, 38, killed by police sharpshooters, it said. He had barricaded himself off on the roof of a downtown building in Cincinnati. He had with him two high-powered rifles and 250 rounds of ammunition. Sniping down into the busy downtown traffic, he killed three people and wounded seven others before being killed himself.

And all I can think to add to this is what my mother said when, eager young journalist I had become, I phoned to ask her to repeat the story I remembered her telling of Ricky, to enlarge on it. More methodical story chaser then, I began by asking her how she had first met Ricky. She paused a few seconds before saying anything, longer than necessary, I thought, for a simple background detail on a long distance call I'd foolishly charged to my own phone. Then she told me, things which shouldn't have been a surprise, which weren't to some important part of me, but did curious things to my breathing, the breathing of son and reporter, and that of the child I had been up until that time at the bridge and who still existed somewhere.

It wasn't much, this new information she gave me, nothing I couldn't have guessed for myself. It required a leap back in time for me to comprehend it, which turned out to be not much of a leap at all. It required that I remember back to when my mother used to spend time in her rock garden, humming to herself as she planted or weeded next to the tall weeds that were the Wilson lawn. That was easy enough; I remembered it clearly from my childhood. It required I go back before then though, that I put up a fence strung between elm trees to separate the two yards, ours and the

Wilson's, which wasn't there as far back as I remember. And it required that I envisage my mother as she was just after she was married, before I was born, when she wasn't much more than a girl herself.

When my mother was this age she hadn't much more to keep her occupied than her diligent attendance of the garden in the backyard, for my father was already a six-day-a-week salesman, a veteran who had been fighting hard for years to support his mother and the infirmed stepfather he had by then; to put aside enough money to one day marry, though he hadn't known then whom it would be. My mother was several years younger than he, a Prairie girl from a small farm come east to work. I think, knowing my father, that he must have felt quite lucky to have her. I know he never allowed her to work during their married life. During those first winters she prepared suppers for the two of them, cleaned the small brick house, subscribed to the Book-of-the-Month Club. During the springs and summers she had the garden.

My mother said it was a long time before she actually met Ricky. She said that for weeks he would come and just stand at the fence, watching her, and though he was big for his age, he must also have been abnormally shy, for he would never reply to her occasional comments. She said it was only after this long and silent introductory period that she finally did coax a few words from him, and the relationship or friendship — I forget exactly what she called it — began.

Yes, I can only guess, reconstruct. He told her, of course, about his ambition to play big league baseball, explaining after they got to know each other the intricacies of pitching curves and spitballs; told her of girls he was interested in at school — for he was precocious, unshy, at least in this area, at least in the talking about it, at least with my mother. These facts I know, details passed on in the form of cute anecdotes, the form itself passed on by a tradition which never had been enough to contain my mother's material. And another fact I know: he must have shared her pregnancy with her, with me, at least part of it. I have worked out the times: when Ricky was eleven or twelve, I was just being born. This occurred to me suddenly, talking to her later on a visit home; and her thoughts must have been running fairly close to my own: for a moment it was as though we searched each other's face for signs of a third, some other, something to contain a closer than mother-and-son connection. We could easily have talked of my father then, relaxed ourselves into something large and sad and blurred. But we didn't. There was something too out-of-scope to all that, and the story wouldn't let us. It would have required changing hats.

She told me, finally, during that phone call, that Ricky's father used to beat him, as though that should explain everything. And later, visiting her, she told me again, ending the story with the slightest gesture of her hands, as though, like it or not, this was the final truth, and what else could she say?

And it was the final truth, for her, and finally for me, which is what is important. And there was little else she could have added. What point could there have been to mention that Ricky's father disapproved of his spending so much time leaning against the back fence talking about God-knew-what to the pregnant neighbour-woman? What point to say that Ricky was punished for this, or that my father knew and also didn't like it (out of jealousy? concern for Ricky? who knows?) or that, if these were true, she continued talking to the boy anyway? She didn't say that she knew of Ricky's plans to steal the guns ahead of time — no doubt she didn't — or that she was in some way involved, if only as a potential audience for tales of the exploit after it happened. She didn't say that Ricky's father almost beat him to death, after the police visited that day, cracking ribs and blackening both eyes — a family friend happened to mention this detail to me during my visit home, later. And I understood no more fully.

Finally, my mother never said whether she and Ricky ever spoke again after the incident, during the four or five years following, till Ricky would have been sixteen or so and I remember her, irrevocably mother and wife; during the time when the elms must have come down, succumbed to disease. And but for Ricky's means of death and my mother's — what? tone? the accumulation of sound which was her voice, as she told her story? Yes, but for these two, and a third: my mother's too-complete understanding as I told her my own story, of the buzzing, the bridge, relating this all to Ricky — how I could *almost* understand how the whine of his day-to-day life in the factory could become a hum, then a voice, talking, directing; how the voice could become impatient — for it is always impatient — and decide that something, even the wrong something, is better than the watching, waiting: nothing: pretending to be interested in a different game. But for these, I would have said that for the next four or so years, Ricky and my mother never spoke again across the lot line — as I'm sure they did not. That there was no further talk of big league baseball or girls. That my mother never crossed over from our property — as she certainly ought not to have done, for whatever reason — or wanted to. And but for these — Ricky's death, the sound of my mother's middle-aged voice, her too-easy comprehension of mine as it creeps towards middle age — I would have said that it made no difference.